JERZY

JERZY

Jerome Charyn

Bellevue Literary Press
NEW YORK

First published in the United States in 2017 by
Bellevue Literary Press, New York

For information, contact:
Bellevue Literary Press
NYU School of Medicine
550 First Avenue
OBV A612
New York, NY 10016

Library of Congress Cataloging-in-Publication Data
is available from the publisher upon request

Bellevue Literary Press would like to thank all its generous
donors—individuals and foundations—for their support.

 This publication is made possible by the New York
State Council on the Arts with the support of Governor
Andrew Cuomo and the New York State Legislature.

 This project is supported in part
by an award from the National
Endowment for the Arts.

Book design and composition by Mulberry Tree Press, Inc.

Manufactured in the United States of America.
First Edition

1 3 5 7 9 8 6 4 2

paperback ISBN: 978-1-942658-14-6

ebook ISBN: 978-1-942658-15-3

Contents

MR. CHANCE ❧ 9

LANA, 1969 ❧ 89

DOWN ON THE FARM, 1967 ❧ 131

LITTLE RED ❧ 167

MOSES AND GAVRILA, 1944 ❧ 195

JERZY

MR. CHANCE

– 1 –

~

Before there was Kosinski, there was Peter Sellers. I wouldn't have known anyone without Pete—not Stan Laurel, not Princess Margaret, not Mr. Chance. I'd met Sellers in '63, when he was the darling of film producers. Every studio wanted him after *Lolita*. There wasn't a comic role that Pete couldn't play. He was Laurel *and* Hardy, a fat boy who could glide around in a thin man's bod. But if you loved him in *Lolita* as the demented playwright, Clare Quilty, please look again. Sellers *was* Quilty, whose saraband of voices and masks camouflaged a murderous rage. He threw a chair at his first wife and threatened to kill her. He threatened his own darling son and daughter. And he threatened me.

"I'll maul you, love. I'll do you in."

His great-great-granddad was Daniel Mendoza, one of England's most beloved boxers, the first Yid who had ever had an audience with a British sovereign, and Pete's megalomania had convinced him that he was as burly as Mendoza. But he knew that my own granddad, Archibald Diggers, had once been lord of the London docks. And that's how come Pete had hired me in the first place. I was an Anglo-American stranded in New York, a journeyman actor, playwright, and philosopher who was driving a limousine to pay the bills. And Sellers told my boss that he would allow no one but Archibald Diggers' grandson to chauffeur him around Manhattan.

"Ian," he said, "I want to kill a man."

I'd seen him as Quilty. And I'd pissed away a fortune on acting classes. I decided to go along with his riff.

"Right, Mr. Sellers. Kill a man."

"I want you to run him down. Knock him off at the knees."

"Will you sit up front with me, Mr. Sellers? Or hide in the backseat?"

"Hide? I wouldn't miss it, love. It's a lark."

It was some Hollywood mogul who had slighted him, or what Sellers imagined as a slight. This mogul was staying with his wife at the Pierre, but he had a mistress in SoHo. And Sellers and I lurked outside a loft on Leonard Street in my company's Lincoln Continental. The mogul's name was Garganus, and he was the fattest man I had ever seen, fatter than a sumo wrestler, fatter than Orson Welles. Garganus must have had a glandular problem. But I didn't hold it against him. I had no grudge against fat men. It was his mistress who fucked with my head. Her fatal flaw was that she reminded me of my wife—blond she was, a real looker, and all legs.

I gunned the motor. I had little to lose. I couldn't get into the Screen Actors Guild, and my wife had left me for a furniture salesman. I had as much rage as Clare Quilty. And Sellers could sense that. It excited him. He seemed in a trance.

"Calm yourself, Ian, like a good little lad."

"I'm going to kill that fat fuck," I said. "I'll knock him and his tart off at the knees. He'll shed a few pounds . . . and Blondie won't be so tall."

A fat man himself, Sellers sank behind his horn-rimmed glasses.

"Someone is bound to recognize me. I'll be ruined. And what

about my mum? She'll have to tell all her mates that her own boy is a homicidal idiot. Be a good lad, Ian. Drive away, drive away. I'll reward you with a bonus."

"Mr. Sellers," I said, "if I can't kill him, then I might as well kill you."

We were inseparable after that. He took me everywhere with him, even to Hollywood. I was glad to leave Manhattan and the specter of my wife. And I didn't mind Sellers' little insanities. He claimed there was a woman at the airport who was hexing us and giving him the evil eye. He wanted to cancel our flight, but I calmed him down. We were going on a pilgrimage to seek out Stan Laurel, who was hiding somewhere in L.A. Sellers' cadre of international detectives couldn't locate Stan Laurel, couldn't seem to find his address. Stan had dropped out of sight after Ollie's death, in '57, and swore never to perform in public again. But Sellers was obsessed with Stan. His fortune-teller, a certain Mrs. Murray, had predicted that he would never make his mark in films until he met Stan Laurel.

He wouldn't sit down with studio execs, wouldn't go through the gate at Paramount until Stan had blessed him. Meanwhile his managers worried about the revenue they would lose while Sellers searched for an invisible man. But they were all wearing blinders. I found Stan Laurel in the phone book. He was living at a seaside resort in Santa Monica. I talked to him on the telephone. He was modest and shy, but said he would be happy to sit with Sellers.

Pete had rented a bungalow at the Chateau Marmont, where Brando used to dwell, according to Mrs. Murray, so Sellers wouldn't hear of staying at any other dump in Hollywood. Soon he mesmerized the entire hotel—Sellers had a way of stunning you. That was his genius; that was his maddening gift. He had turned himself into Marlon Brando in front of our eyes, but the metamorphosis was so subtle, we had little time to reflect. Suddenly we had Marlon Brando where Peter Sellers had been. The lethargic man in horn-rimmed glasses glided and slid like a cat. He might have usurped Brando's midwestern drawl. But that would have been much too simple for Clare Quilty, who could imitate any voice. He was silent, but when he had to talk, he talked like Pete. And that was pure devilry, as if Marlon Brando, for the unique pleasure of the Chateau Marmont, were playing Peter Sellers.

When I told him about our appointment with Stan Laurel, he wasn't particularly pleased.

"What, that old tit? Why should I bother with him?"

Then his mood shifted yet again. He began to fawn over me, like a child who had just been slapped.

"Mustn't keep Stan waiting. He's my idol, you know. I'd watch him and Ollie for hours. Couldn't get me out of the picture show. We were stuck in Ilfracombe during the blitz. Mum had moved us out of harm's way. And all that sea air made me ropey. I was used to the greasepaint and sweat of the music hall—Mum had her own act. She played the Ratcatcher's Daughter, and other choice roles. And now all we had was sun and sea. And so I crept into that comfy tomb of the local movie palace. And there in the dark was Stan, with his wimpy voice that could comfort a lad who'd been the only Jew at St. Aloysius'. Mum thought it best to send me to a Catholic school, you see, so I could learn the catechism. Priests made the best professors, Mum said. No one bothered calling me Peter. All they had to say was 'the Jew.' I was one of a kind. I could have murdered Mum. But I hugged her for half an hour, thinking murder. 'My darling,' I said, wanting to bite into her throat and silence her forever. And it was Stan Laurel's whimpering that kept me sane. There wasn't another funnyman on the planet who could weep with a smile on his face. And I'm here to pay homage to Stan. Come, boyo, I'll wash his feet."

He wouldn't consider renting a car. He'd had his Bentley Continental shipped over from London—he was always buying and selling premium cars. He sat up front as we rode out to Santa Monica Bay.

"I'm so excited," he said. "If you're lying, Ian, I'll beat your brains into pulp. Stan will really see us? I'll die of shame if he sends us away."

He kept up this riff until we arrived on Ocean Avenue; then he turned silent. I could sense his sour mood; his whole bod seemed to rattle with rage. Anything could have triggered this transformation—the hint of salt in the air, the jolt of some lost memory, or an overload of random static inside his head. I saw nothing that should have alarmed him, nothing but a harmless row of resorts.

Stan Laurel lived at one of these hotels, which had an enormous swimming pool half a block away from the ocean. But I couldn't taste the sea. The air on Ocean Avenue had the sweet smell of lacquered wood.

Pete wouldn't get out of the car. He dug his shoulders into the Bentley's expanse of cushions. It was like being lost in a caravan.

"I can't face Stan," he said. "I'm all knackered. I'm done in."

"I'll knacker you in a minute if you don't crawl out of that bus."

He was whimpering, in Stan Laurel's voice, but I hardened to his magic and hauled him from the cushions.

"You're a monster, you are. I'll have you arrested for assault. Your granddad was a murderer, and so are you. . . . Can't you see, Little Ian, this bloody place reminds me of Ilfracombe. It has the same sickening sweet smell, the rot of old wood and bitter, broken lives. I'll never make it inside. I'll start to puke."

"Then I'll give you a tin can to puke in."

And I shoved him past the rotting doors of Stan's hotel. The lobby looked as if a hurricane had hit it; pictures of the sea hung from crooked nails in the walls; chairs and tables tilted at an impossible slant. The hotel clerk stood behind a desk that seemed about to cave in. He had an intercom that was composed of snaking wires with silvered tips. He plugged one wire into a metal board, whispered a few words into his own fist, and announced that we could go upstairs to see "Mr. Stan."

Stan Laurel looked like an aging child in a sweater that was much too small. He lived in an apartment that seemed to fit perfectly with his own size. He'd been given an Oscar in 1961, for a lifetime of clowning, and the statuette sat on a desk laden with lamps and assorted bric-a-brac. And the moment we arrived, Stan pretended to polish the statuette with his sleeve. It must have been part of a comedy routine he'd prepared for pilgrims such as ourselves. I'm sure he didn't have the vaguest idea who Peter Sellers was.

He was blinking and smiling at us in the middle of his routine, when suddenly his little red eyes seemed to pop out of his skull. Pete had grown enormous, stood like a giant who was much too large for Stan's living room.

"Babe," the little man whispered without his famous falsetto. "Babe, is that you?"

Sellers didn't answer him at first. He'd turned himself into Oliver Hardy in the middle of Stan's blinks, but Hardy without a mustache, or bulbous cheeks and a bald crown.

"Stanley," he said, "where is my breakfast?"

The little man started to cry. "I'm so happy," he said. He shook my hand, but he didn't dare approach this phantom who talked like Oliver Hardy.

"Must I repeat myself?" Sellers said with one of Hardy's signature smirks. "Will I have to wallop you?"

"Please, please," said Stan. "I haven't been walloped in years."

And then he went into his old weeping act. The big fat man had always made him cry.

"Ollie, I don't have a thing in the house . . . not the butter you like. I haven't shopped once since I moved to Santa Monica. The bellhop always fries my eggs."

"And what if I discharged the bellhop and fried your head in the griddle until your ears started to explode?"

"Oh, I would love it, Ollie, I really would."

Stan hopped around his cluttered room in ecstasy. I worried that he would have a heart attack. But I couldn't slow him down.

"Mr. Sellers," I said, nudging the big fat phantom. "Do something. He'll hurt himself."

But Stan himself came to a stop. And he had that pixieish grin of a shrewd performer; he's the one who had invented Laurel and Hardy's little ballets. "Thank you for coming. Too bad I don't have any tea in the house. Would you like my autograph . . . and a picture of Babe and me?"

And that's when I really took my measure of Pete; the whole aura of Oliver Hardy vanished from his face; he shrank into his own skin.

"No," he said. "The pleasure of meeting you was enough. I shan't forget it."

"Forgive me. I can't recall your name."

"It's a trifle," Sellers said. "It has no significance. We'll be on our way."

"But do come again. Next time I won't forget the tea."

Sellers was seething by the time we left the Oceana Hotel.

"You were marvelous," I said. "For a moment you had him

fooled. He looked so depressed, so shrunken, when we came in—a relic in his little room. And then his eyes lit. He really thought his old partner had come back to life. His face was on fire. It was kind of you, Mr. Sellers."

"He gives me the creeps. Do I want to end up in some dungeon by the sea? Fondling a statuette? No thanks. You can cross Stan Laurel off my list. I'm sorry you ever found him."

And I drove Peter Sellers back to studioland in that silver Bentley of his, while he sat in utter silence.

— 2 —

~~

I THOUGHT HE WOULD SACK ME, squeeze his eyes shut and cast me adrift. He had his own entourage, a mob of sycophants, including a chauffeur, a secretary, and a bodyguard, and I wondered why he would need another waif.

"It's your looks, Ian, it's your looks. A handsome bloke like you. It calms people, puts their fears to sleep. And all the birds are attracted to you. They're drawn to you like flies, and I'm not greedy. I'll settle for the slop that washes ashore. Besides, I could use a reader. I'm sort of illiterate. But you mustn't tell a soul."

I'd studied James Joyce at school, but as Peter Sellers' reader, I had to read *Ulysses* again. He'd been asked to play Poldy, Leopold Bloom. I relished the idea of Peter Sellers as Poldy. He would have heaped upon Bloom some of his own comic madness and quicksilver. But he changed his mind at the last minute. *The Pink Panther* had ruined him. The whole world wanted him to repeat the role of that bumbler, Inspector Clouseau. He wasn't an actor anymore. He was a fucking franchise. But he did have the most loyal of fans, Princess Margaret, who loved to do her own impersonations of Inspector Clouseau.

The royal family had picked up Peter Sellers, had adopted him, like some toy dog. He could be outrageous at Windsor or Clarence House and Kensington—spill his soup, tug at the tablecloth, or ride from room to room on the tea trolley, bumping into the palace chamberlain. The queen thought he was the funniest man alive. But it was her sister, Princess Margaret, the wife of Lord Snowden, who understood the sadness behind his savagery, since she was something of a toy dog herself. She had been performing since the age of two. She was the little sister, the *unserious* one, while Elizabeth Alexandra Mary, or "Lilibet," was born with a scepter in her tiny fist. Lilibet had been reared to rule, while Margaret Rose, who was twice as beautiful, had to cross her large crystalline eyes and play the clown at her side. And thus she was fond of Peter Sellers, as one clown to another.

"I'm nervous, dear boy," he crooned. He had this cockeyed scheme of marrying Princess Margaret and moving into Kensington Palace. He continued to plot, even while Snowden, famous as a fashion photographer, was one of the few friends he had; they would go off together on long photographic safaris; still, Sellers plotted behind his back.

"Ian, PM doesn't love that pygmy. They fight all the time. God's my witness, I watched her make a fist and knock him down. PM's a better prizefighter than Mendoza."

"PM" was Princess Margaret, of course. She was also called "Ma'am." But Sellers loved to call her "Ma'am Darling."

"She's spoiled rotten, Ian. She won't leave the palace without her detective and her chauffeur. Can you imagine having dinner at Raffles or some other bloody trattoria with a detective from Scotland Yard breathing down your neck? How could I propose marriage?"

"She's already got a husband, Pete."

His eyes began to hood over with malice. "Don't you ever call me Pete again. I'll cut your heart out and feed it to the lions, I will."

"But your mum calls you Pete all the time."

His mouth started to quiver. "Leave Mum out of the picture, boyo."

"But she's already in the picture, *Pete*."

She would arrive at the Dorchester, where we were holed up, because Pete would rather live at a hotel than in his penthouse near Hampstead Heath. And his mum was always coming upstairs to visit in her toreador pants, her hair dyed orange or purple, depending on the season or her mood. She'd hug both of us for half an hour. "Peg and Pete," she would coo, "Peg and Pete against the world . . . and now Little Ian." He'd bought his mum a flat in Highgate, but she couldn't resist the Dorchester, with its liveried butlers, who would always greet Peg with a long hello and squire her to Sellers' door, clutching a golden cage. Peg went nowhere without her parrot, a gift from Pete. The parrot was known as Henry, which was Pete's middle name. He'd been born Richard Henry Sellers, but Peg had a little secret. She'd had *another* boy, named Peter, who had died as an infant while she was on tour. She almost never spoke about him, but Pete had inherited that dead boy's name. He was the living ghost of an earlier Peter Sellers. That was why he had such a weakness for astrologers and other clairvoyants; they nourished his belief in reincarnation.

But I didn't learn about that dead boy from Peg or Pete—it was from the parrot. When Henry wasn't screeching "Bollocks" or "Bugger off," he would cluck his tongue and ask, "Where's the dead baby, where's the dead baby? Where's Peter Sellers?"

Pete would cover the cage with a kind of blackout cloth and threaten to hurl Peg's parrot off his own balcony at the Dorchester. "Down to Hell with him, Mum. I promise you that." She'd start to cry and plead with her son. She'd already tossed back enough scotch to drown her parrot.

"Henry's all I have, love. . . . I lost my other boy. I was at the music hall, wearing a white tutu, when he choked to death. He swallowed his own bile. Greenish it was. I will never forget that color. . . . Pete, give us a hug. You and Ian are good boys."

I'd have to drive her home in the Bentley he had bought for his mum. His dad, Bill Sellers, had died in '62. I was bowled over when I saw a picture of Bill. He looked exactly like Pete. He'd run off with another bird during the blitz. Peg had to take him back, like she would a wayward boy. She slept in the same room with Pete. Bill was banished to the sofa in the sitting room. He was the lone Protestant in a tribe of Sephardic Jews that loved to squabble.

And now I was squabbling with a maniac who was descended from Mendoza.

I promised not to call him Pete in front of PM.

"But why would you want me at Ma'am's garden party? I'm a bit short on royal blood."

"But you're a reader, *my* reader. And I wouldn't want Ma'am to consider me obtuse. She's friends with Gore Vidal and all those literary barracudas. PM can spend a whole afternoon in bed with bloody William Blake. And I can't read his poems. They bore me. So you're my shield, Ian. You'll protect me from her darts. When she starts to recite about burning tigers, just chime in. I'll slowly slip into your shoes and become William Blake in front of her eyes."

His astrologer had warned him that he had to woo Princess Margaret this month. And it was best not to interfere with his madness. I wore a velvet suit to Kensington Palace and a black silk shirt. Pete wasn't bothered at the gate, but I had to deliver my passport to a clerk, who squinted at me and checked my name off a list. Ma'am's own detective, a bloke with enormous hands, kept my passport in his pocket.

"Hello, Mr. Sellers. Is this your man?"

"Yes, Burroughs, and you mustn't be rough with him. Ma'am wouldn't like it."

Burroughs accompanied us to the royal tea tent. It was as tall as the palace, and it rattled in the July wind. I grew dizzy watching the tent's tarpaulin skirt sway round and round my head. I didn't recognize any of the royals, but then I recalled that Ma'am and her husband had their own crowd of barracudas—mobsters, models, and musicians, sprinkled with a few of London's literati and notorious hangers-on.

I was welcomed into this club once Pete introduced me as Archibald Diggers' grandson. The London mobsters, who looked like financiers in their Savile Row suits, insisted that my grandfather was the savviest breaker of skulls that London had ever seen.

"A legend in his own time, Archie was. He could split a man right down the middle."

And then Her Royal Highness appeared with Snowden, the commoner who had been made over into a lord. Pete longed to accomplish the same trick, to supplant Snowden and even surpass him by hopping out of the royal box as some prodigious lord of lords. It was a ludicrous quest. He would have been a madman after a month or two of palace life with Margaret.

He was ebullient under the tent, calling her "Ma'am Darling" and kissing her in front of Snowden, who was in the midst of a much publicized affair with Lady Jacqueline Rufus-Isaacs, one of London's tallest and most exquisite beauties; Peter loved to regale me with the story of how he'd once squired Ma'am (and her detective) to some restaurant in Soho and found Lord Snowden and Lady Jacqueline seated at another table. The detective, Burroughs, fell into a blind rage, but Ma'am sat down, nursed her scotch, and said, "Peter, do be funny. I'm in the mood for some fun remarks."

Pete carried on five conversations at once, playing Snowden, Jackie Rufus-Isaacs, Burroughs, Ma'am, and Peter Sellers, excoriating each of them and himself, while Ma'am puffed on her Gauloise in a black pearl cigarette holder and never laughed. Finally she leaned over, said, "You are a darling boy," lured Pete back to her palace, and let him make love to her for the first time, with the detective outside her door. And Pete smelled marriage after one knockabout in Margaret's bed.

She didn't have Jacqueline's long legs and regal bones; Ma'am was barely five feet tall, but she had the pale complexion of a child, with a swan's white neck, a sensual mouth, and blue eyes that crinkled with mischief and warmth. I'd been in love with Margaret Rose ever since I saw her in a newsreel in 1943; she must have been twelve or thirteen when I was six; she was carrying a helmet and a gas mask and wearing a British officer's uniform; she had enormous, smoldering eyes; I believe she was the mascot or honorary colonel of a tank corps, and in this newsreel she was inspecting the tanks. She saluted the tank men. Her voice trembled slightly. "My brave boys," she said, her words sounding like a song.

I had to hide my crush on her while Pete introduced us. I dipped my knees a bit; you weren't supposed to shake a princess's hand. I didn't expect her to smile. But her lips pursed after one look at me and her blue eyes began to glaze. Then she whispered to herself and bolted away. And I realized that Pete had led me into some sort of trap. All that banter about William Blake was a ruse of his. I wasn't meant to talk literature with Margaret Rose. I wasn't mean to talk at all.

Her detective didn't seem to like me, but I had to appeal to his sense of fair play. Burroughs had a bullish neck and bulging eyes. He must have been trying to protect her with his own perpetual scowl. He wore a topcoat in midsummer—I hate to think of the truncheons and pistols he had stored in his inner pockets.

"Mr. Burroughs, sir. Have I wounded Princess Margaret in any way? It was not my intention. I—"

"Are you daft, old son? You remind Ma'am of her lost love."

Half the planet must have memorized her fairy-tale romance with Group Commander Peter Townsend, a fighter pilot who had become an equerry at Windsor after the war. He was sixteen years older than the teenage princess, who lived in her own tower and rebelled against the seriousness of her sister. She must have wooed Peter Townsend with her eyes alone, and that wooing went on for years. And by the time she was ready to marry him, Lilibet sat on the throne. Townsend was both a commoner and a divorced man, and the queen's advisers threatened to take away Margaret's title and her royal allowance if she dared marry Peter Townsend. They bullied her into giving him up. And they'd robbed Margaret, "the Sick Rose," of all her joy. I thought of bloody William Blake. I wanted to whisper into Margaret Rose's ear the song of Blake's Little Girl Lost.

> *Know that in a former time*
> *Love, sweet love, was thought a crime.*

While I brooded, Margaret Rose came up to me with her own silent wind. She seized my hand, held it in hers, and with her other hand she clutched an enormous flute of champagne.

"Dear Mr. Diggers, I cannot forgive myself. I was horribly rude. But will you ever forgive me?"

She was smiling now, and that imperial ice of a princess was gone.

"There's nothing to forgive, Ma'am. I startled you. But it wasn't out of malice. I'd never been told that I bear a resemblance to one of your former equerries."

"Not much of a resemblance, dear," she said, licking the champagne like a naughty cat. "*My* Peter was a thinner man, almost ascetic—but it's your expression that's so similar, like a man who inflicts pain upon himself."

"I didn't realize I was such a flagellant, Ma'am."

"Call me Margaret, please. Margaret Rose. Darling Peter Sellers says you're something of a Blake scholar."

I laughed, and Ma'am seemed to like it. "I'm a failed actor-playwright and a failed philosopher. But there isn't much scholarship in my dossier. Mr. Sellers was praising me—"

"To puff himself up. But there's another party involved in all this intrigue. Your grandfather."

"I'm bewildered. How could my grandfather ever have entered your dreams? Windsor Castle was light-years away from London's waterfront."

"Ah," she said, "but they are closer than you think," and invited me to have a sip. I was even more amazed. I didn't know that a commoner and a princess could drink from the same glass. And while I nibbled champagne, Margaret Ma'am recited William Blake in a voice as soft and solitary as royal velvet.

> *I wander thro' each charter'd street,*
> *Near where the charter'd Thames does flow,*
> *And mark in every face I meet*
> *Marks of weakness, marks of woe.*

"It's not such a mystery, darling boy. My nurse grew up on tales of Archibald Diggers that her father had told her, and she recited such tales to me. I couldn't go to bed without them. I was addicted, you see."

"There were actual tales about my grandfather?"

"Zillions of them, about the lord of the London docks. But Nurse was a great liar and embroidered whenever she could, and in her telling he wasn't a mobsman anymore, but a national hero who fought the enemies of England—terrible chaps who were always trying to infiltrate our shores and take over the Thames. But the marvel of it is that I told Nurse's stories to Peter, *my* Peter, and we never had such laughs. And so when *your* Peter introduced you as Archie's grandson, I suddenly remembered how much I had lost. And I took my fury out on you, Darling Diggers."

A little of that fury must have come back. She grabbed the flute out of my hand, finished the champagne, smacked her lips, and tossed the flute to Burroughs, who caught it without batting an eye. Then, as only a princess can do with a commoner, Margaret Rose raised one hand, rubbed her knuckles against the curious sandpaper of my cheek, said, "Dearest, I was dying to know how that felt," and dismissed me with a final glance.

—3—

SELLERS COULDN'T BEAR that I'd sipped champagne with Ma'am Darling out of the same glass. He groaned like some second-rate tragedian, accused me of undermining his efforts to marry Margaret. His mouth was flecked with foam.

"Did you talk with Ma'am Darling about my prick?"

We were having tea and cucumber sandwiches at the Dorchester. There were wedges of cucumber on his cheek. He would have strangled me if he'd had the strength, strangled me in front of the Dorchester's liveried lads.

"Did she tell you that I was a lousy lay, that my dick's too small?"

"Pete, Ma'am didn't mention a single part of your anatomy."

"Then what did you talk about, love?"

"Archibald Diggers."

"I'm flummoxed," he said. "I'm getting ropey again. Did you tick along with my intended, hold her hand, give her a French kiss under that bloody tent?"

There was no point in trying to reason with him. He was filled with black bile. But I had something to distract him with. He'd gotten excited over a book. It had been recommended by another reader, and Sellers passed it on to me. A short novel by a Polish-American writer who was lionized in literary circles. That would have mattered zilch to Pete. But the language of the novel was so simple, Sellers himself could read it.

He fell in love with Chance, the hero of the novel, a kind of idiot savant who spends his whole life in a rich man's garden. Chance is without an echo, without a single reverberation. His sexual parts never developed, and so he has no longing, no desire. He is a castrato who was never castrated. Suddenly, the rich man who has been caring for him dies, and Chance is cast out of the garden, wearing the rich man's tailored suits and shirts. But he has the look *and* the haberdashery of a banker or business tycoon. And through some trick of fate, he ends up in the mansion of a real tycoon and the tycoon's luscious wife, EE, or Elizabeth Eve. Chance the gardener becomes Chauncey Gardiner in his new home, his only language the language of a garden, yet the tycoon and EE are in awe of him; they have never met someone so emptied of artifice; and they interpret his talk of seasonal growth and death in a garden as images of society itself, until he begins to sound like an economic wizard, a shy but persuasive savant of savants. The tycoon, Benjamin Rand, introduces Chauncey to the president of the United States, who is also mesmerized by the man in the tailored suit and his gardening talk. And soon secretive men in the White House's inner closets decide on Chauncey as the president's running mate in the coming election.

Sellers cried after he read *Being There*, the book about Chauncey Gardiner. He had glanced into the novel's crazy mirror and seen himself. Hadn't he also leapt out of the muck, the lad who had come from nowhere? Chauncey Gardiner was addicted to the tube, watched it day and night, and could mimic whatever action was on the screen. Wasn't Sellers the same sort of mime?

"Ian, you have to get me the rights to that book. Chauncey's the best mate I ever had. Kill the author, I don't give a flying fuck. I'll bury him in Chauncey's own garden."

I could understand Pete's desperation. He'd had a string of heart attacks in '64. His heart had stopped beating for two minutes. And he liked to boast of how he'd come back from the dead. "I was chatting up the angels, love. Sexy beasts they were . . . and then they dropped out of sight, and I was a lad without a point of view."

But those two minutes of suspended animation, of life in death, or whatever they call it, defined his current predicament. When he wasn't playing Inspector Clouseau in yet another *Pink Panther*, he had flop after flop. He blundered along for five more years with his heart's own irregular rhythm. And he saw his chance in Chauncey Gardiner.

But Jerzy Kosinski got in the way. If Sellers couldn't kill Chauncey's creator, he would have to woo him. He began sending Kosinski cryptic cables.

> *Mr. K., won't you let me into your garden?*
>   *—Your admirer, Chauncey Gardiner II*

But he seemed terrified to get on the phone with Mr. K.

"Ian, what will I tell him? I haven't read his other works. I don't know a bloody thing about Poland or politics. I'm Chauncey Gardiner."

"But he might be amused by that."

"No, no. You'll have to call him, Ian. You're the charmer. You'll analyze his bloody book. What else am I paying you for? You lout, you stinking kettle of fish. I'll have you banished from the Dorchester. You'll have to grub on the streets, show your arse on Petticoat Lane."

I called Mr. K. I couldn't charm him at all. He talked to me as if he were interrogating a prisoner of war.

"Who are you? What do you want?" he asked in the clipped accent of some phantom secret service.

"Sellers," I said, "Peter Sellers, he wants to play Chauncey Gardiner."

"Are you his *law*yer, his theatrical agent? Where are you calling from?"

"London," I said. "I'm calling from Mr. Seller's suite at the Dorchester."

"What's outside your window?"

"Hyde Park," I said. "The Serpentine. I'm Mr. Sellers' literary adviser. I entertain him when I'm not telling him what books to read."

"Why does he harass me with cables and wires?"

"He doesn't mean to harass. He fell in love with Chance the gardener. I told you. He wants to—"

"That's impossible," said Mr. K.

I was beginning to feel as crazed as Clare Quilty. "What's impossible?"

"Chauncey Gardiner is not for sale. Sellers would drown him in slapstick. There are no pink panthers in my book. I have my own ideas about the film. I intend to play Chauncey Gardiner. You can go to the devil with your Mr. Sellers."

Pete flew into a rage when I told him he couldn't be Mr. Chance. He began to tear up his suite at the Dorchester. The hotel managers had gotten used to his tantrums. But I was sick of Pete. And whenever he flared up, I would disappear from the Dorchester and walk to a pub I knew near Holland Park. I was having a snack of buttered brown bread and bitters at a little place on Duchess of Bedford's Walk when someone tapped me on the shoulder. It didn't feel like a friendly tap. I whirled around with a snarl. "What's your problem, mate?"

And I looked under the rim of a bowler hat, into the preternaturally large brown eyes of Ma'am's detective.

"Come with me, my son."

− 4 −

I WAS SHOVED INSIDE A REAR DOOR at Kensington like some clandestine on a risky mission for the Crown. The cluttered warrens I saw must have been the servants' side of the palace. It was a miracle: I'd gone from the Dorchester to Charles Dickens in less than two hours. I thought a cyclone had crashed through these rooms and robbed them of intimacy or charm. Mr. Burroughs, the Scotland Yard man, led me onto a car that was like a dumbwaiter meant for two; our knees touched, and the edge of his bowler caught under my chin as we traveled aloft with a series of shivers.

We landed in a dark corridor, and I kept banging into boxes and abandoned bedposts; we must have stumbled upon Kensington's secret storage bin. The detective had his own flashlight, his little torch, and he led me on a merry chase until he stopped in his own tracks, knocked on a door, said, "It's me, Ma'am," and let me into a room as large as a barrack, but this barrack was cleared of debris. It had Chippendale dressers and chairs, armoires and mirrors laden with chinoiserie, and a bed with pink pillowcases and a pink coverlet. The princess sat on this coverlet in a black silk slip. She was biting into her black cigarette holder while she stared at the vault-like ceiling of her own royal barrack. Her skin was deliciously pale, her arms plump as a white peach. But I wasn't blind to the purpose of this place. It was where Ma'am held all her trysts. The princess couldn't rent a room in Notting Hill or Earls Court to meet her lovers. But why had I been summoned here? We weren't in the midst of some splendid, impossible passion. We hadn't even begun the least little dalliance, except for the fact that she had rubbed my cheek under the royal tent.

Finally she looked down from the ceiling. Her blue eyes were dead.

"Dickie, is that you?"

"No, Ma'am," muttered the detective. "Dickie's in Argentina. You sent him away, remember? He stole from you and your niece, cropped a necklace from the Queen Mother. I had to dislocate his shoulder to get it all back."

She laughed, and her eyes grew alert with a sudden wisp of memory.

"Yes. 'The loot,' you called it. 'We have to get back the loot.' But you never smile, Burroughs. Not even when we have our victory. And whom have you brought, Mr. B.? Some stud from Sadler's Wells? A professional gigolo you found in the street?"

"No, Ma'am. It's Little Ian. You asked for him yourself."

"Archie Diggers' boy?" She clapped her hands. "I command you, Burroughs. Bring him here, else you'll forfeit life and limb."

"Why not forfeit *my* life and limb?" I asked, without moving an inch closer to Margaret.

We were far enough away from the bed so that Burroughs could whisper, "Careful, my son. Ma'am has one of her migraines."

He seized the scruff of my pants and carried me like a parcel over to the bed. The spectacle must have amused her.

"Burroughs, you may go now. I'm sure to be safe around Little Ian."

"But suppose he steals the crown jewels, Ma'am?"

"I'm his crown jewel," she said. "And Little Ian has my permission to steal me."

The detective sulked and crept like a panther out the door.

"I won't bite," Ma'am said while beckoning me to sit beside her. Her bed was strewn with books. And it was no light summer reading list. I recognized *Lolita, Mrs. Dalloway*, and *Being There*.

"Ma'am, did you fall in love with Mr. Chance?"

Her eyebrows knit, royal eyebrows that had never been plucked or penciled in. She bit into her black holder; there wasn't even the trace of a cigarette at the other end. I must have puzzled the princess. Her eyebrows knit again.

"Don't jolly me, Little Ian. I'm not in the mood. I cannot recollect meeting Mr. Chance."

"He's the gardener in Kosinski's book."

"Glorious," she said. "*That* Mr. Chance. Lilibet lent the book to me. She has no time to read. She has to hunt deer in her favorite forest and meet with the prime minister. She's always conspiring with her ministers. I have my own spies at Windsor, you know, even if I am a penniless princess who has to rely on Lilibet for her allowance. And what am I now? A harlot, with poor Burroughs as my pimp."

Ma'am reached over and slapped my face.

"Don't you dare pity me. I will not allow it. . . . I told Lilibet about that gardener, said she would have a few jollies reading the book. But you are fiendishly clever to ask, Ian. I do have a terrible crush on the gardener. Both of us grew up behind a glass wall, watching other people cavort. When I married Tony, I rode to my wedding in a glass carriage, the little girl of glass who could watch Lilibet's subjects watching me. I wished to God that I could shatter before the wedding took place. . . . Are you appalled that Mr. Burroughs kidnapped you?"

"He didn't kidnap me," I said.

"He most certainly did. Those were his exact instructions. 'Uproot Ian from wherever he is and bring him to the slut of Kensington Palace. Discretion advised, but use force if necessary.' I am shameful, Ian, am I not?"

"Yes."

"I ought to be spanked. Will you spank me, Ian?"

"No," I said. "I will not spank you, Ma'am."

"Will you make love to me, then? It's purely medicinal. Rutting with a man is a remedy for migraines."

She looked away from me during that little speech. Her lower lip was trembling. I wanted to touch her, take Ma'am in my arms, drink the salt from her eyes, but I didn't dare. I had no silly dream of riding in a glass carriage and becoming the duke of Kensington Gardens. I'd been in love with this royal wench since I was a child and saw her in the movies with her gas mask. But it wasn't so simple a matter to rut with Margaret Rose for medicinal purposes.

"Damn you, Ian. Do I have to beg? I fancy you. Isn't that enough?"

Margaret slid out from under the straps of her slip—Lord help us, she was white as milk. Ma'am never moved once, never stirred, as I rose above her. Then her eyebrows suddenly knit, her entire torso swayed, she screamed like a little girl startled by the sound of her own delight, licked my face once, and fell fast asleep.

～

B URROUGHS WAS WAITING for me outside Ma'am's door in his bowler hat. We plunged into the bowels of Kensington Palace again, and exited from a different gate. He had no more sympathy for me than he might have had for a worm.

"If you show up at the front gate asking for Ma'am, my son,

you'll not have a very long life. You are to forget about this excursion, remove it from your mind."

I had to devil him, get under that smug mask of his. "What if Ma'am should ever ask for a repeat performance?"

He snorted at me. "Ma'am never asked for you. You were the first available lad I could find. She's in a haze when she has her headaches. I was pleased that she could come out of it long enough to remember your name. And if you try some funny stuff, like extortion, my son, Special Branch will put you on the next plane. Show me your pockets."

That miserable detective patted me down smack in the middle of the palace garden. I felt like a convict.

"Tell me what you're looking for, Burroughs, and I might be able to help."

"Duke of Verdura diamonds," he said. "The last one of Ma'am's admirers stole a Verdura brooch in the shape of a camel's back. Took me a year to track it down. But I wouldn't expect an uncouth lad of your nature to comprehend the duke of Verdura. He was an aristocrat from Palermo who never designed for Philistines, never sought fame. When you wear a Verdura, you wear it for life."

He delivered me to the Dorchester in Ma'am's Rolls-Royce and sent my carcass out the car door.

— 5 —

I MIGHT HAVE RUN TO THE PALACE and shouted "Margaret, Margaret" from the princess's lawn, but it was Sellers who saved me. He had read in some London rag that Ma'am Darling had listed Chauncey Gardiner as "the most delightful character I have ever met in a novel, after Mr. Micawber and Sancho Panza."

And so he dispatched me to the States to meet with Jerzy Kosinski and convince him to offer Pete the chance to play Chauncey Gardiner. It was like a curious game of cat and mouse, where I was the mouse who had to court Kosinski. Every time I called, he said, "You again? The pest who belongs to Inspector Clouseau."

But after the fifth or sixth call, he took some pity and gave me an appointment. He lived near Carnegie Hall in a two-room flat that was like an animal's lair with a bit of light. And I wasn't startled at all to discover that he resembled a dapper bird of prey, with piercing dark eyes and a prominent beak.

I hadn't been idle. While he kept me on a string, I devoured *The Painted Bird*, the novel that had helped create Kosinski. It was utterly removed from *Being There*, a book with a disembodied voice that could have crept out of a machine. *Being There* was a perfect vehicle for Mr. Chance, who lived in another man's hats and suits and had no discernible history other than the reflection in his eyes from flickerings on a little screen. But the anonymous boy who narrates *The Painted Bird* is awash in the muck of human history. His voice has a cruel, relentless beat. He's six years old at the beginning of the novel. It's 1939, and we're in an Eastern European country that has just been occupied by the German war machine. The little boy comes from a large town, where he had a privileged life, with a nanny and lots of books. His parents have sent him to a remote village away from the war. But the woman who was meant to care for him dies after two months and the boy is suddenly adrift. He looks like a Gypsy, or a Jew, with his dark eyes and olive skin, but is surrounded by blond, blue-eyed peasants who cannot read or write and call him "the Black One," akin to the devil.

The boy endures a pandemonium of punishments as he wanders from one remote village to the next. He's beaten many times, left to drown in an ice hole, hung from the rafters of a barn, with a murderous dog baying at his feet; petrified after being thrown into a manure pit, he loses the power of speech. The only ones who are ever kind to him are monsters of a sort, outcasts like himself, the disfigured and the damned: a half-witted bird catcher; a voluptuous giant of a woman, Stupid Ludmilla, who lost her reason after being raped by a gang of drunken peasants; and Ewka, a skinny farmer's daughter with a goiter growing on her neck, who reveals to him all the curious perfume and spit of lovemaking; but the boy feels betrayed by Ewka, after he catches her coupling with a goat.

Yet this goiter girl's fascination with a goat troubled me far less than the image of a painted bird. Lekh, the bird catcher, who was in love with Ludmilla, liked to paint one of his prize birds in all the colors of a rainbow and send it back into its flock; the other birds would stare at this decorated creature, refuse to recognize it as one of their own, fall into a rage, and peck it to death. The little boy also sees himself as a changeling who has to avoid being pecked to death by his own kind.

And so when he is reunited with his parents at the end of the war, they feel as foreign to him as the blue-eyed peasants. He has remained a bird-boy, a freak, with savagery as his own real education; he himself is forever secretive and cruel, with cunning as his protective color. And the Mr. K. I met in his dark Manhattan lair was a grown-up replica of that bird-boy.

The lucky ones, like Kosinski, had survived the war through subterfuge and by adopting the cruel tricks of their tormenters until it was a kind of second skin. And this was the skin that Kosinski chose to wear *with* his blue blazer. The author of *The Painted Bird* greeted me with the cockiness and clipped accent of an SS captain.

"Tell your master that Mr. Chance is all mine—who are you? What do you want from me?"

"Nothing," I said. "I'm a fool on a fool's errand."

"Where are you from?"

"Nowhere," I said.

His voice softened, and the SS captain suddenly went into hiding somewhere. Mr. K. invited me to sit down, but there was precious little place to sit. His lair was cluttered with cameras and tripods and other paraphernalia. He offered me vodka from his fridge but wouldn't drink with me, and I had to slurp my Stolichnaya all alone.

"Alcohol is poisonous to my system. The first drink could be fatal. You'd have to call an ambulance. . . . Tell me your name again."

"Little Ian." That's what Pete and Princess Margaret and her detective in the bowler hat loved to call me.

But the bird-boy in the blue blazer was a whole jump ahead of Pete.

"Little Ian Diggers, whose grandfather was the holy terror of the London docks."

I began to stutter, and I had never stuttered before.

"My grandfather isn't even known in the United States. Who t-t-t-told you about him?"

"Peter Sellers," he said like a mountebank, or a hissing snake that had delivered me into a trap. "Your master was quite explicit. He phoned me twice yesterday, talked about your esteemed grandfather, said you yourself were homicidal when you did not get what you wanted. You're Sellers' slave . . . and his attack dog."

"Like Judas," I said.

Kosinski smiled; that smile was much more sinister, and much more cold, than the carapace of an SS captain. Judas was the name of the devil dog that had nearly bitten off the little boy's legs in *The Painted Bird*.

"Comrade, I can see that I'll have to be twice as careful with you now, or you'll use my own words against me. But your master was clever in his own stupid way. He'd roused my interest, not in him, or his obsession with Mr. Chance. My gardener is a gaunt man, not a fat, four-eyed comedian. But I had to know if you had inherited your grandfather's violence. My hand was shaking when the doorman announced you. Not out of fear, but excitement. I wanted to learn what our chance encounter would bring."

"Then I'll probably disappoint you," I said. "I'm not violent, and I'm not sure that my grandfather was. I think he used violence as a technique to stun his enemies on the docks into obeying his commands. He killed when he had to kill. I suspect he was rather cerebral."

"As real assassins are. They kill with economy. The rest are commonplace, and not worthy of our time. But I'd be willing to bet that you have the complicated clockwork of a killer. And if the right occasion arose . . ."

I didn't have a minute to catch my breath. He invited me to a cocktail party given by Senator Lionel Jaspers, the last great liberal Republican in Manhattan's sea of sharks. Without the Democratic machine to bind him up in corrupting cables and cords, he had the aura of a saint. Besides, he had a wife who could dazzle most men. She was a Polish Scheherazade from the Lower East Side who had been born into great poverty and had married a political prince. Together, Jaspers and his beautiful witch of a wife ruled over Manhattan's high culture. There wasn't an emerging young playwright, dancer, novelist, painter, architect, or musician who hadn't been celebrated at their table. They had a penthouse on Park Avenue that was the most selective salon in Manhattan. Annabelle (née Anita) Jaspers was seldom seen at Senator Jaspers' Georgetown "palace." She preferred the electrical storm of Manhattan; and the senator, despite his brutal schedule, preferred to be with his Scheherazade.

I wasn't surprised that Annabelle had adopted Jerzy Kosinksi, had welcomed him into her entourage. No American novelist could ever have had Kosinski's éclat. He owned the authentic stink of *Mittel* Europe, had survived the Holocaust as a bird-boy who had lost the power to sing or fly. But I didn't belong at Annabelle's salon.

"I'm Sellers' slave. You said so yourself. Annabelle's butler won't even let me through the door. And I have nothing to wear. I'm not dressed right for a band of cultural barracudas."

"Shush! You can be my date."

He disappeared into a closet and came out with a double-breasted Prince of Wales coat that must have cost a fortune. He insisted that I wear the coat.

"You'll be smashing," he said.

I looked in the mirror and all I saw was another bird-boy.

−6−

I T WAS THE MOST EXCLUSIVE ADDRESS on the planet: 740 Park
Avenue, so exclusive that sometimes it was masked by another
address, 71 East 71st Street, where the building had another
entrance. Jacqueline Kennedy had spent her childhood here,
together with a cornucopia of tycoons. When it was no longer
fashionable to have a mansion on Fifth Avenue, millionaires
moved their "mansions" indoors to 740 Park, with fountains and
marble staircases and duplexes with twelve full baths and twenty-
five rooms, according to Kosinski.

He puffed out his chest and boasted that he had once lived at
740 Park. I didn't believe him. I couldn't reconcile his bat cave with
some apartment as big as a bowling alley. But when we got there,
the building's slew of doormen accosted him as if he were their
own lost king. Not one of them called upstairs to Scheherazade:
they didn't have to announce the coming of Jerzy Kosinski.

And he was greeted like a king by Annabelle and her guests,
half of whom had the hawkish look of hunger artists. I tried not
to stare at Annabelle. My awkwardness must have amused her.
Scheherazade smiled. She was succulent in her black dress. There
was no other way to describe her. She had curly brown hair,
with ringlets over one eye, and a sultry, pouting look reminis-
cent of Claudia Cardinale. But the senator's wife reminded me of

someone else—Stupid Ludmilla in *The Painted Bird,* before she had been raped by a gang of louts and lost her mind. Annabelle and Ludmilla had the same ripe flesh, I imagined, with a musk that could dizzy a man.

But Scheherazade had guzzled too much champagne at her own salon; she swayed in front of us while she squinted at me.

"Jurek," she growled, "who is this boy?"

"My Boswell," Kosinski said.

Nothing registered in her enormous myopic eyes. "Which Boswell? Does he dance for Balanchine?"

"He's my biographer, Nita darling. He's writing a book about me. I met him at Yale. Professor Diggers. But you mustn't flirt with Ian."

"Flirt?" she said with a ferocious laugh. "I never flirt."

She stole me from Kosinski and plowed across the living room with her arm around my waist, and paraded me like some magnificent monster from Yale, where Kosinski himself had been made a fellow at one of the colleges, a few years after *The Painted Bird* was published.

"Meet Jurek's Boswell," she said. "A famous biographer. He's working on a book about our dark-eyed wonder. He'll crucify me, I'm sure, turn me into a notorious nymphomaniac, and poor Lionel will be drummed out of the Senate."

Several heated faces pressed close to mine and commiserated with Annabelle.

"Nita, he wouldn't dare," the hunger artists tittered. I didn't even mind their mocking tone. I was too involved with Annabelle's aromas, and with her hip bone thrust into the small of my back like a delicious knife.

And then Annabelle went off with her little band of artists and abandoned me to all the other barracudas. I wasn't distraught. *The*

Painted Bird had provided a key to Kosinski, and all I had to do was turn it once or twice. He'd come out of the war as the captain of his own secret service; that was how he managed to survive. If he was a changeling, a bird-boy, he incorporated whatever peculiarities he had into his own myth. He must have been plotting to leap into a salon like Annabelle's since the age of seven. Writing novels was only a tiny portion of his secret service.

Once Annabelle's hip bone vanished from my back, I bore into him like a bird-boy of my own. I watched. He was the jester king of her crowd, entertaining Annabelle's suitors and sycophants with tales of his childhood.

"Yes," he said in that clipped voice of the SS captain. "I was mute during most of the war. But there was a curious reversal once I was reunited with my mother and father. They had hidden themselves, and their lives had narrowed down into the dull belief that they had disappeared. They weren't wanderers. The war had turned them to stone. I had lost my nanny and my books. I didn't read one word while I was on the run. But I had to read the hate in a dog's eye and the eagerness of some ignorant farmer to annihilate me because he despised the swarthiness of my skin. It was my survival kit. And when my mother and father found me, I saw in an instant that I had become *their* parent, that I had sprouted a porcupine's quills while they shrank and shrank. I was armored and they were not."

But there were inconsistencies in the fabric that the jester king had spun, little bumps in the fiction. And one perceptive listener began to finger his jaw.

"But why would your parents need porcupine quills, Jerry? They weren't Jewish."

It was another of Kosinski's fables that he'd been baptized before the war, when it was apparent from the rudest reading of *The*

Painted Bird that the little boy with the Gypsy eyes had come from an educated Jewish family in Warsaw or Lodz. I was willing to bet that a Lower East Side witch like Annabelle must have sniffed his Jewishness but allowed her jester to keep his Catholic mask.

He gathered in his shoulders and answered his acolyte.

"The Germans wouldn't leave my parents alone. My father had made remarks against the Nazis. He had to hide. He was an intellectual, a mathematician, and my mother was a concert pianist. But she couldn't play in public. She had large breasts, and they embarrassed her. They would begin to flop and jiggle while she played, and she couldn't bear it. She retired from the concert halls, sat at home while my father did his calculations and I scratched the alphabet on my slate. . . . The sound disturbed my mother. She had sensitive ears. It was swimming that consoled her. Mama loved to swim. But she had the same predicament at any seaside resort. She was convinced that everyone, even the little girls, stared at her breasts. She would lie under her blanket until it was dark and the beach grew deserted. Then she would make a dash into the water and whisper to me across the waves. 'Jurek, where are you?'"

"But darling, don't lie," said Scheherazade, who had returned to the side of her jester king. "Jurek, how could you hear your mother whispering from the water? Was she the siren of Cracow?"

"Lodz," said Kosinski. "We lived on Gdanska Street, in Lodz. And my father had an automobile, an *Amerikanka,* it was called, because it had an American motor. He sold textiles when he wasn't solving mathematical problems or teaching linguistics, and he had to travel from town to town, but when my mother had a sudden, irresistible lust to swim, he would drop his textiles and drive us halfway across Poland to the Zanzibar, a little resort hotel on the Baltic Sea.

"We were pensioners at the Zanzibar. Sometimes we would

remain for a month. My father would play games of chess against himself, assuming a different personality whenever he pushed the white or black pieces, and I could no longer say which *self* was really his. He could change his persona, according to which side of the board he was on. It was camouflage, a way of blending in. My mother did not have that gift. She was solid and willful, and wouldn't have known how to play a chameleon."

"Don't torture us," Scheherazade said with a pout, plucking at her own curls. "For God's sake, what happened to your poor mother on the beach?"

He was silent for a moment, relishing the static he had created. The war had turned Jurek into a storyteller whose mission it was to reshuffle things until his entire history was obscured.

"Nita, *nothing* happened on the beach. After the other bathers went away and we were alone, Mama would dance in the water without a stitch of clothes. She wasn't ashamed when I looked at her breasts."

"How dare you!" Annabelle giggled and growled. "Jurek, you were too young to have an erection. You couldn't have been much older than four."

"Hypocrite," Jurek hissed at her. "I've seen you bare your breasts in front of your own little boy."

"Only to educate him, darling . . . about a woman's parts, and not until he was nine or ten. But your mother was perverse. Seducing a five-year-old."

"You're wrong. She sat in the sea and pretended to play the piano on an imaginary bench. It wasn't seduction, darling. Mama was sharing her performance with me."

"And what did she play?" Scheherazade asked in a hoarse whisper.

"Chopin," he said. "The concerto in F minor. I caught every single sound."

"That's preposterous," said one of Annabelle's protégés, profoundly jealous. "Jurek is trying to bewitch us. Not even the Baltic Sea can capture a sound that doesn't exist."

"I trust him with my life," said Annabelle. "Feed us, Jurek. And silence this fool. How could you tell what your mother was playing?"

"By the movement of her hands on the keyboard."

"There was no keyboard," her young protégé smirked.

"Shut up," said Annabelle. "And leave this house at once."

She took Kosinski's hand and led him into her own labyrinth of rooms, shutting every door between her and ourselves.

⌐⌐⌐

I WAS SURPRISED WHEN JASPERS HIMSELF invited me to spend the weekend at his beach house in the Hamptons. The senator and I had never met before, but we sat on his sundeck like a couple of conspirators, sipping our vodka tonics. He was goggle-eyed, like a great big frog, with spindly arms and legs and a swollen chest that beat under his polo shirt with the force of a second heart. His father had been a tailor in Manhattan who specialized in chauffeurs' uniforms, so how did Lionel Jaspers get so rich? It was rumored that his money came from the Shah of Iran, that he was little better than a secret agent for the Shah. All I know is that he was madly in love with his wife.

He followed her every move with his goggle eyes. His son, Lionel Jr., was away at summer camp. But Lionel Sr. couldn't have Scheherazade to himself. She liked to live within a whirlwind of other men. And this weekend was a whirlwind of one—Kosinski.

The senator seethed in his deck chair and suddenly attacked.

"You're Jerzy's jackal, aren't you? You help him with his filthy deeds and then dust up and get rid of all the traces. I hear you come from a long line of hit men. You know, I was the first to sponsor Jurek. I gave him his start. I introduced him to Hank." The senator could see my perplexed look. "*Hank, Hank,* you idiot. Henry Kissinger. Hank is fond of that Polish Houdini, says Jurek's a treasure, a real find. But he ignores it when Jurek and Nita play footsies under the table."

Jurek seemed to steer away from Annabelle's own tempestuous path while we were out at the Hamptons. He was too involved with his "comet." It was a miniature make-piece stove that consisted of a tin can punctured with holes and filled with smoldering leaves and wood, attached to a length of wire that he would swing like a lasso until it shot sparks of fire into the air that resembled shivering stars. Such a tin can had been the most important apparatus in *The Painted Bird*. A comet had kept the little boy from starving. He carried it everywhere. With it, he could heat potatoes that he took from some farmer's bin. He could fight off dogs and gangs of wild boys with a judicious swing of his fiery can.

And Jurek didn't abandon his comet, not even when Annabelle appeared suddenly in a straw hat and a one-piece black swimsuit that was meant to eat into our hearts. But she didn't twitch her tail or smolder like a femme fatale. She walked an unwavering line to the beach and stood in the water as stern as a schoolmarm. I couldn't fathom her little parade until I realized she was luring Kosinski away from his comet with her own bag of tricks. She didn't conjure up an imaginary keyboard and pretend to play Chopin on the Baltic Sea with her breasts bared, as Jurek's mother, Elzbieta, had done. She just stood there in her black tank suit and Jurek *smelled* his mother. He dropped his magic stove and went down to the water, as if in a trance. The power of his tale about the Baltic had emboldened her to be Elzbieta. Jurek was caught in his own trap. Scheherazade had diminished the storyteller, turned him into a child.

The senator sniffed the sea air with bitterness, his frog's eyes appearing to pop out of his head.

"I can put you on my payroll . . . as my confidential secretary on the Hill. I wouldn't ask you to spy. I'm not interested in the sordid details, Ian. I want to make sure that Nita is safe. Will you tell me if he tries to hurt her? I hear he pulled a gun on some guy who objected to the portrait of Polacks in one of his books. I could have had Jurek thrown out of the country, but the son of a bitch became a citizen a couple of years ago. I could still have him thrown out, but Nita would have a fit and find another Polack with skinny shoulders who can build a storm inside a tin can. You aren't a novelist, are you?"

I didn't have to answer, and what could I have said? That I was a footloose jackal in the employ of Peter Sellers.

The senator wouldn't have understood a word. And how could I ever console him? Jurek and Annabelle were locked in an embrace that didn't require tongues and spit and private parts. He might have howled with displeasure had he caught them copulating like a pair of wild dogs. But *his* Scheherazade would never have captured him in a primal tale of mother and child. Lionel wasn't a storyteller. He was a politician who could swat at his opponents until they were paralyzed with fear. But I doubt that he could ever have stood in the sea with Annabelle and fallen into the same sort of trance.

−7−

~

WHILE JUREK WAS IN THE WATER with Annabelle, and the senator watched with his frog's eyes, I devoured *Steps,* Kosinski's second novel. It was even more frightening than *The Painted Bird*: The nameless bird-boy has grown into a monstrous storyteller whose disparate tales are like a series of steps toward oblivion; the narrator is trying to erase us as he erases himself, but he leaves several smudges, his own marks in the mirror, which become points of navigation put there to preserve our sanity.

If we stare into the mirror long enough, we catch Kosinski at his sleight of hand, and realize that the war has robbed the bird-boy of his childhood: He's become a golem without a human guide, bereft of pity and remorse; and this relentless book takes us right inside the golem's head. We are lost, horrified, as the narrator relates to us his cruel seductions and tricks: The tale of Ewka, the goiter girl, coupling with a goat in *The Painted Bird* bothers us, because we know that the little boy is in love with her, and craved her touch. But the echo of that scene in *Steps,* where a peasant girl copulates with a large animal as part of a private show, leaves us bewildered, because we cannot locate a point of view. The narrator sees everything around him as a spectacle, and while the peasant girl screams in pain, he imagines that her suffering is part of the show.

I wasn't accustomed to the disconnection I had experienced in

Steps. But Kosinski's own contours become recognizable after a while—the boy who weaves his way through a deadening Communist regime in Poland and arrives in America wearing an overcoat of Siberian wolf fur that shrinks in the rain, who wanders through supermarkets stealing black caviar, becomes an outlaw cavorting with outlaws, dreams of inflicting punishment and pain, of littering highways with a load of bent nails and watching as the cars crash.

The bird-boy lost his soul sometime during the war, just as he lost the power of speech; and the sounds that come back to him later like some ghostly boomerang have their own lamentable music. The narrator he will become in *Steps* begins to haunt a sanitarium for patients with tuberculosis; he makes love to one of the dying women by staring at her reflection in the mirror; he photographs her naked body, and tries to imagine his own face in the reflected image of her flesh. A nun at the sanitarium accuses him of being a "hyena," who feeds upon the dying and hastens their death.

And Kosinski's staggered, unadorned music had crept out of a golem and a ghoul. It was the mark of his writing, with its sunless territories and stark furniture. Wasn't Mr. Chance a kind of ghost who was shoved into the land of the living and finds it even more somber than his own existence? And so was Sellers. He was constantly lamenting about his own immaterial being. "I'm a ghost, love. I'm gone, departed, unless I play a part."

He went from role to role, but even then he was diminished and mummified. He faded more and more each time he was Inspector Clouseau. And I was hoping that Chance might revive him, that he might rediscover his own lost face inside the flesh of Kosinski's gardener. But I couldn't get him that role by badgering Kosinski. The best attack was no attack at all.

I did not mention Pete's name once in the Hamptons. I read my book, tore into the charred steaks that Jurek prepared on the senator's fire, drank vodka tonics with Frog Eyes, watched Jurek twirl his comet, wondering if those sparks could conjure up a Polish wood? Or was it another manipulation of that man in *Steps* who liked to photograph dying women?

Where was the baroness who was supposed to be his companion? Frog Eyes kept talking about her while we fed like vampires on our bloodless steaks. He was very drunk. "You've been hiding the baroness again, you rogue. Jurek, I can't play chess without the baroness . . . unless you care to play."

The bird-boy stared at him. "I abandoned chess years ago, Senator. I played against my father in Poland. He wanted to make me into the grand master of Lodz. But I refused. He locked me in the closet."

"When was that, darling?" Scheherazade asked, pretending to nibble at her steak, which had the consistency of burnt cardboard.

"Weeks before the war," he said. "My governess would implore him to let me out of the closet. 'Not until he promises to play,' said Papa. And so I played with him, plotting my revenge."

"Darling, you can't mean that," said Annabelle, her own eyes swelling with mischief.

"But I did. I picked up the game after the war. My father became a minor official in the Polish Workers' Party. Papa so much wanted to blend in. He would rise within the party by never making a single demand for himself. We had our own car and driver. But Papa suffered several heart attacks and was soon pensioned off. He saw this as a godsend. Now he had all the time in the world to tutor me in chess. But photography was my passion, not black and white queens. I was in high school and went chasing after girls. I would win over the prettiest ones by asking them to pose for me.

But Papa tried to interfere. He said I couldn't wander around Lodz with my camera as a weapon. I had to stay home after school and memorize the moves of earlier chess champions. We got into a fight. He ran and hid inside the closet. It wasn't the same closet where he had once locked me inside. We now lived on Senatorska Street, in the spacious quarters of an ex–party official. But I hadn't forgotten that dark place of punishment. Papa had terrified me, had once made me whimper, and promise to become his own little chess champion. Now I heard him tremble in the closet. I would have kept him in there for months, fed him little scraps under the door, forced him to piss and shit on a great pile of clothes. But Mother cried that he would have another heart attack if I kept him in there too long. I couldn't bear to watch her beg. I unlocked the closet and let the pensioner out, the mathematician who wanted to turn his own son into a chess problem."

"For Christ's sake," said the senator, "I can't digest my food with all that palaver. Just tell the baroness that I would love to play chess with her."

Jurek went on grilling more steaks à la Kosinski, a skill he had picked up from Polish peasants while he was a little vagabond. He allowed the steaks to "marinate" in a bed of dried leaves that built up an archipelago of smoke and smothered the meat. The peasants must have used that trick to disguise the taste of rotten meat in war-torn Poland. But Jurek had twisted their piece of adversity into his own primitive cuisine.

O N THE WAY HOME TO MANHATTAN in his customized Buick with tailfins and a bumper of metallic teeth, he still wouldn't talk about the baroness. He invited me to visit him the very next evening. His front door was open when I arrived.

I walked into the apartment but couldn't find Kosinski. Manuscripts and photographs were strewn about, and though I didn't mean to pry, I was riveted by the woman in the photographs—all were studies of the same face in varying degrees of agony. The woman possessed a stark, painful grandeur. I couldn't discern the color of her hair or eyes; the shots were in black and white. But the photos seemed to chart the woman's disintegration; in several of them her hair had begun to fall out; in others she had a lion's mane and a piercing smile, as if she were showing off her defiant love for the photographer; in some her eyes were hollowed out and her cheeks sucked in.

I panicked for a moment, wondered if I were witnessing an act of necrophilia. Was she the sick patient from *Steps,* the woman he had photographed in a mirror during the various stages of her "death"?

I began to hear a rasping noise, like a rodent in the room.

Then someone called to me in Kosinski's voice. "Ian, will you let me out of the genie's jar?"

I believed him. *A genie's jar.* But I couldn't find the genie. Then I noticed that one of the drawers in the dresser beside the rear wall was wiggling. I opened the drawer. Kosinski was lying within, all folded up, like a sweater or a shirt.

He unfolded himself and crept out of the drawer.

"My God, how could you accomplish that?"

He smiled à la Kosinski, with his tight, narrow mouth. "You're my Boswell. Can't you guess? . . . I was hung from the rafters of a barn when I was a little boy. My shoulders were dislocated. But there was an advantage in that. It made me double-jointed, like an acrobat."

"But we're not inside a circus. Why the hell would you hide in a drawer?"

"There's a price on my head. I have enemies among the UB, the Polish secret police. I flirted with the bastards once. That's how I got out of Poland. They forged documents for me, from institutions and professors that do not exist. And they felt betrayed after I published my first books. They had considered me as one of their sleepers, and when I wouldn't perform for them, they decided to kill me."

I didn't believe a word of it. "I'm not with the Polish Gestapo, Jurek. How come you hid from me?"

"I wanted you to gaze at the photographs without any distractions."

"Is she the dying woman in *Steps*?"

"No, she was a mistress of mine, a salesgirl at Bendel's. I met her while I was buying an expensive monogrammed scarf for the baroness. The salesgirl helped me pick the scarf. I trembled in front of her eyes, told her I had to photograph her or I would jump out of my skin. I begged her to leave the store that very moment. She did."

I was the one who was trembling now. "What was her name?"

"I called her Evelyne. She liked that, the anonymity of it. She was a born actress, my Evelyne. She loved to pose. She undressed even before I asked."

"But where did you photograph her?"

"Right here, in this room, with a huge black drape over the windows and reflectors on the walls. She stood with her hands over her head, her armpits adorned with rich red hair, like roughened silk with a waft of sweet perfume. I had never been so aroused by hair on a woman's body. I was drawn to her like a lovesick moth to a red flame. But she wouldn't let me kiss her or bury my head in her armpits until I finished our session. The spotlights and panels of silver foil excited Evelyne; she licked her lips every time I leaned over her with a lens. And she insisted that we make love under the lamps and the silver foil, a hidden camera clicking with its own time delay."

"And did you grow weary of your new model?" I asked, dreaming of her rough red silk.

"Not at all. I couldn't get enough of Evelyne. But she wouldn't tell me where she lived. She would meet me in a month, she said, show up at my door. But if I should follow her, or seek her out at Bendel's, she would quit her job, and I would never see her again."

It sounded like a suppressed chapter from *Steps,* but I couldn't stop listening.

"She had changed, wilted in a month. That wild perfume was gone; the red silk under her arms was all matted now, like dull fur; she was still eager to have me crawl over her with my camera; and there were little ravenous moans with every click. But I couldn't have sex—that underarm silk had served as an amulet, a love ticket, and now nothing she did could please me."

"Jurek, did she turn away from you?"

"No," he said with a wistfulness that seemed to crawl right out from under that secretive mask of his. "It was like a marriage in which she was faithful once a month. . . . Had I imagined the red silk, created my own jungle creature with a magnificent splurge of hair?

"She continued to knock on my door. Each time I photographed her under a blitzkrieg of lights. I began to feel stuck in some strange pietà, where I was murdering my own mother, punishing her for having aroused me at the Zanzibar—it was on the Baltic, while we were bathing, that I first discovered the luxurious red hair growing under my mother's arms. It was our very own secret, outside Papa's realm."

"What happened to Evelyne?"

"She disappeared, didn't knock on my door; I missed the companionship we'd had under the lights. I felt closer to her than any other model I had ever had—the waifs I'd met at parties, the prostitutes I'd picked right off the street. But I wasn't idle. I looked for Evelyne everywhere. I even played policeman. I returned to Bendel's wearing a military uniform. I love uniforms. I collect them. I could show you my closet, Ian. I have epaulets and insignias that would oblige a Turkish general to kiss my feet. I discovered the power of a uniform in Poland. Sometimes a silver mark on your shoulder can make the difference between life and death."

I growled at him. "Jurek, please. *Evelyne*."

"I must have interviewed ten salesgirls. They were enchanted with my uniform and would have done anything for me. I talked to the manager, described Evelyne—it's another trick I learned in Poland. The best lies keep as close as possible to the truth. I elaborated a little, of course, said I'd come to Bendel's a year ago to buy a scarf for my fiancée, when I suffered an attack of vertigo. One of the salesgirls had been kind to me, sat me down with a cup of water, selected the scarf, and—"

"Were you able to find Evelyne?"

"The manager had no record of her. She wasn't in Bendel's books. But I took advantage of my epaulets. The manager became my mistress."

I didn't want to listen. But the son of a bitch had captured me like a conjurer. I wondered if *Evelyne* was nothing more than a wisp of smoke that had come out of his comet. It didn't matter. I was deep within his thrall.

— 8 —

~

W E WOULD PROWL AT NIGHT, Jurek insisting that we carry
black masks. There was nothing unusual about them.
They were party masks that one could buy at the five-and-ten,
with cardboard nose cones and deep eyeholes—the typical fare of
a phantom secret service. But Jurek's mask did seem sinister, and
I'm not sure why. Perhaps it was the way he wore it, at a wicked
slant that revealed one of his nostrils. People shouldn't have been
menaced by half a nose, but they were.

We rode to East Harlem in his Buick well after midnight. I
didn't want to get out of the car. We'd arrived at a fleshpot on
116th Street, a farmers' market of male and female prostitutes
with a flock of admirers and pimps. I saw policemen wearing
chains, drag queens who could break your heart, revelers who
pissed on the sidewalk, men who walked their dogs, women with
biceps as big as ostrich eggs.

"Jurek, we're the only ones with masks."

"Shhh," he said. "The mask will save your life."

He plunged into this carnival, and I felt a strange tranquillity
in him, even with half his face masked. He moved with a kind
of exalted freedom, and I realized that the bird-boy had come
home. The anarchy on the street must have reminded him of his

childhood in the midst of war. These night crawlers could have fallen out of a Polish forest, or drifted into *The Painted Bird*.

The entire population saluted him.

"Hi, Pluto baby, how ya been?"

"Hello, Sarah darling. . . . Hello, Joshua," he whispered, walking among his subjects.

He seemed to know everyone's name by heart. He dispensed money and advice like a lord of the underworld. He exhorted, cajoled, danced with a drag queen in the middle of the street. He didn't have a camera, didn't want to photograph freaks at a private zoo. He wasn't a storyteller here, entertaining Scheherazade's guests. He was Pluto with his people.

I had never liked him until this moment. I adored *The Painted Bird* and Mr. Chance, not the man of calculation and ice who had created them. Now there was warmth beneath the eyeholes of his mask. He wasn't distancing himself, observing from the rooftops, mocking his own creation.

"Pluto doesn't need a bodyguard," I said. "Why am I here?"

"To watch my back."

"But they love you, Jurek. Let's dump the masks."

"It soothes them," he said. "They don't have to watch my eyebrows, interpret every wrinkle. They would attack us, I swear, if they had to look at my face for very long. I'm Pluto. That's enough."

But there was a sudden frenzy. The drag queens and the prostitutes began to scatter. Some hid behind Pluto; others ducked into alleyways. Two men had arrived in a battered green Ford. They must have been undercover cops who considered this carnival as their own turf. But something was out of kilter. I don't mean the earrings and other paraphernalia of cops in disguise. These cops wore lipstick and eyeliner, and had white powder on their cheeks. They called themselves Mabel and Madge.

"Mabel, look at what the cat dragged in. Pluto and his punk. Should we arrest ol' Pluto or kick his ass?"

"We'll give him a warning, Madge. He has to collect his shit and never come here again with his punk."

My instinct was to run right out of Harlem. But Pluto was enjoying himself. He laughed into the murderous still wind that Mabel and Madge had brought with them.

"Darlings, I'm not moving. And you ought to be gracious enough to leave. You're not wanted here."

Mabel and Madge had blackjacks that were like rubber snake heads on a spring. They twirled the blackjacks and flicked them in front of Jurek's mask.

"One shot, Pluto. That's all it takes. You'd be crippled for a couple of seasons, crippled for life."

I was a bouncer before I'd ever been Pete's slave. I was familiar with blackjacks and the harm they could do. Madge wasn't boasting. A blackjack could turn your brains to putty. But Pluto was reckless in his underworld. He tried to knock the blackjack out of Mabel's hand. Mabel struck him on the shoulder, and Pluto's knees collapsed. Then Madge twisted him around with a shot on the other shoulder. Pluto's eyes wandered under his mask. They meant to humiliate him in front of his subjects, drive him to the ground and have him scream for mercy.

"Darlings," he said, blood spurting from his nostrils. "You can do better than that."

Madge and Mabel hit him again.

I removed my mask. The eyeholes had cut into my peripheral vision. I hit Madge once, twice in the face. He had a startled, moronic look before he tottered and fell, but I hadn't been alert enough. Mabel's blackjack landed on my right elbow, which dropped at my side like a deadweight and dangled there. A nauseating numbness seized my gut. But I didn't faint. I sucked up that nausea and decided to come at Mabel with whatever little I had left.

Looking into my eyes must have confused him. He didn't find much fear, and his curiosity had slowed him down. I clipped him with my left elbow before he had a chance to strike. The black-jack dropped out of his fist. He fell beside Mabel. I picked up the blackjack and hammered every finger in his and Madge's right and left hands. They were beyond the need to whimper. I wanted to break their necks. And that's when I saw Jurek slumped over, catching the bloody strings in his mouth with the cup of his hand, a religious fervor in his eyes.

"I was right," he cackled. "You do have the clockwork of a killer."

Six drag queens appeared out of the dark and began to paw Pluto and wipe his blood on their blouses. They sobbed for him and shrieked their delight. The blood seemed to electrify them. But Pluto hadn't bothered to notice. He was still cackling at me.

God knows, I was drawn to this underworld. I had to get the hell out, or I might have been stuck forever in Pluto's forest. I returned to London on the next flight.

— 9 —

A S USUAL, SELLERS WAS ON THE ROAD TO FOLLY. He'd settled into a castle outside Dublin with a new wife, Miranda, an aristocratic lady who must have reminded him of Ma'am Darling. But Miranda was more interested in her pet birds and dogs than in Peter Sellers. She fed her "babies" the finest fillet, while Pete, the master of Carlton House, County Kildare, had to fend for himself. It wasn't Kensington Palace Gardens, where he could entertain lords and commoners alike under the royal tea tent. In Ireland, he was a jester king without an audience. He grew murderous in his isolation. He smothered Miranda's cockatoo and drowned one of her babies in the pool. He cut off most of his hair in a botched attempt to disfigure himself.

I found him at the Dorchester, where he was hibernating while his hair grew in. He looked dreadful, with patches growing out of his bald pate like twisted wire. But the exiled master of Carlton House took me in his arms and started to cry.

"I was going dotty, mate. Suicidal I was, abandoned by kith and kin."

Kith and kin. He had children he never saw, and three wives, but his mum was his only kin, and Peg had had a heart attack in 1967. She told her nurse to piss off and died in her hospital bed. He hadn't been so kind to her near the end. Once he moved into the Dorchester and began to court Princess Margaret, Peg became an encumbrance with purple hair and toreador pants. He had her cremated at Golders Green—that was five years ago—but he communed with Peg's spirit. He wouldn't start the day without talking to his mum; he could conjure up her voice at will, and Peg advised him about his finances and his love affairs. I wondered now if it was Peg who had made him cry.

I began to feel awkward in his arms. He was hugging me the way Peg had hugged him, with violence and a touch of treacle.

"What's wrong, Pete?"

"Look at me. I can't even stand in front of a mirror. I'm bloody Vincent van Gogh, a walking pot of mutilation. . . . I called Kosinski."

Pete stopped crying and let out the chuckle of a bad little boy. "I chatted him up like a house on fire. I fooled that puss pot. I borrowed your voice, love. He was in bliss. Said he couldn't wait to see you. You both have some unfinished business, says he. Something about a girl in a photograph. Evelyne or Elizabeth—and Pluto. Who the fuck is Pluto? I brought up Peter Sellers. And here's the gist of it, love. The puss pot is coming to London with his inamorata."

I was bewildered. "The baroness?"

"Yes, yes, the baroness. Or some other tart. And I had you, dear Ian, invite them for a romp at the Dorchester in my name. Cocktails in our suite, says I in your best accent. Sizzling steaks and a side salad at the Dorchester grill. We won't even have to leave the hotel."

"Did you mention Mr. Chance?"

"Did I not? He's been scribbling in the dark, practically has a finished scenario of the book, with lots of delicious dialogue, and guess what? He's bringing it with him to London."

CURIOUS AS I WAS ABOUT THE BARONESS, I still dreaded meeting Jurek on Pete's turf. He ruled us all the minute he arrived. He was wearing the same double-breasted suit I had worn at Annabelle's soiree. The baroness wasn't as sultry as Scheherazade. She had short hair and a mannish face. She towered over Jurek in her leather suit, her legs like a lovely pair of scissors. I liked her a lot. I would later learn that they had met at a masquerade ball. Jurek had dazzled her, and she'd fallen in love with him by the end of the ball, discarded the man she had meant to marry, moved in with Jurek, put his filing cabinets in order, typed all his manuscripts, and made herself indispensable.

Before we had a chance to say hello, Jurek tossed us out of the living room, had us close our eyes, and challenged Pete.

"I'm going to disappear, and if you can find me, Sellers, you can play Chauncey Gardiner in any film made from my book."

"That's a lark," said Sellers, not knowing how diabolic Jurek could be. "You ought to tell your solicitor that you've been cheating yourself."

He wore a wig to cover up the twisted wires of hair on his scalp. He wouldn't have seen Jurek without that wig, but it didn't match the gauntness he'd been cultivating as Inspector Clouseau. His face seemed lost under the wig's magnificent pompadour.

The baroness stood behind him with a look of pity on her face, while I opened drawer after drawer in the living room and never found Jurek. We searched every closet, every cabinet, crawled under the couch; he'd folded himself somewhere beyond my ability to imagine.

Sellers stifled a sneeze. "I'm all knackered, mate. My nerves couldn't stand another minute of this."

He plopped onto the cushions of his velvet couch, beckoned us to sit beside him, and had one of the Dorchester's liveried footmen serve us champagne.

"To Chauncey Gardiner," he said, clinking glasses with the baroness; he'd already shoved me into the background. "Tell me, Baroness, does he always play hide-and-seek?"

"Almost always," she said, her knees higher than Sellers' chin. "Once, there was a colonel from the KGB, a defector, who found him. But the colonel had been training spies at a KGB kindergarten for years."

"Ah, then I shouldn't feel so sad. I can't compete with a KGB kindergarten."

He didn't see a hand begin to snake around his ankle, but I did, and I felt sorry for Pete. Suddenly his eyes had a yellowish cast. He froze on his cushion.

"I'm getting the heebie-jeebies. There are rats running around at the Dorchester, rats and other hairy things."

And when that same hand slithered up his leg, Pete rose out of the cushions with a terrible wail. His wig fell off, and he had to cover his scalp with both hands. Jurek came out from under the cushions, where he'd been hiding like some perverse flattened submarine.

"Sellers," he said, with that familiar smile of an SS captain, "you failed the test. How could I trust you with Mr. Chance?"

Sellers had retrieved the wig, but he hadn't had the time to coif it, and it sat lopsided on his head, the pompadour over one ear.

"Couldn't I have a look at the screenplay?"

"No," said Jurek, grabbing the baroness by the hand. And he turned to me with a brutal stare.

"I found Evelyne by sheer chance. She was back at Bendel's. . . . She had never left. It was her hiding ground. She's married to one of the store's executives. And she goes slumming from time to time, takes the place of a sick clerk. I began to shiver the moment I saw her. I had to sit. It was like my first encounter with Evelyne. All her loveliness was there again, that same rough silk in her hair. She didn't have to take any risks. Bendel's was her private brothel. It kept her alive. Male shoppers would fumble around in a women's department store like fish out of water; it was Evelyne who smiled at them, put them at ease, played the innocent whore."

"That's sensational," said Pete, who pushed aside his pompadour, desperate to enter Kosinski's tale. "We'll work her into the script. Chauncey will visit Bendel's after he's thrown out of his garden; he'll buy some trinket from Evelyne. It will be a perfect cameo for Sophia Loren."

Jurek ignored his chatter.

"I didn't even attempt to catch her eye. What was the point? To win Evelyne back and have her decompose under my lens? It was my camera that had been killing Evelyne—it soiled her, took her outside her playful seduction at Bendel's. I'd broken the simple cord of her life. . . . I was in love with Evelyne. That's why I left her alone. Not for her sake, but for mine. I couldn't experiment with her, reenact the same poses under the lights."

He walked out of Sellers' suite with the baroness, while I wondered what kind of romance she'd had under his lens. But I had the feeling that he'd never photographed the baroness, or she would not have been able to last. There were no killer cameras in Kosinski's studio. It was the man behind the camera who killed.

I listened to Sellers sulk.

"I'll never be the gardener. . . ."

And then Jurek suddenly reappeared, smiling like a fiendish cat.

"Peter darling, did you know that Little Ian saved my life?"

Pete had a brooding, murderous look. "That wanker isn't supposed to save your life. It's not in his job description."

"Two crooked undercover cops were bludgeoning me to death. I could hear the devil call my name—that's how far gone I was. And Ian demolished them, shades of his grandfather. He broke their hands. They'll never be able to clutch a gun again . . . or a blackjack."

"And why were these crooked cops after you, love?"

"I'm the patron saint of prostitutes. But that's not important, Peter dear. We now have irrefutable evidence that Ian will go all the way."

"Go all the way?" Pete asked, as bewildered as ever.

"Don't fret. He wouldn't bash his own employer. But you might pay him to silence your enemies—or silence me, for that matter. But it wouldn't get you a mite closer to Mr. Chance."

And he was gone again, like some irritant, some pestilence put there to infuriate Peter Sellers.

—10—

~

I WASN'T CLEVER ENOUGH TO KEEP PACE with Pluto. He'd written *Being There* as the skeleton for a film script. That's why the novel seemed to lack an interior life. It wasn't out of Chance's apparent aphasia. It was the reductive language of a screenplay.

Perhaps the scenario itself had been shopped around. All I can say is that Sellers wouldn't give up. He had a pacemaker sewn into his chest; he suffered from periodic fainting spells, worried that the simplest cough might provoke a heart attack, but he was determined to play Mr. Chance before he died. And he did. Kosinski relented after six years. A deal was put together, and filming began in January 1979 at Biltmore House, a castle in North Carolina that had once been the most humongous private residence in the United States; even its current keepers couldn't recall how many rooms, turrets, and dungeons Biltmore House had. It was the summer residence of the Vanderbilt clan at the beginning of the last century, with more than 100,000 acres, and now it was a gigantic movie prop.

Pete had never allowed me on the set of his other films, but he'd consulted with his mountebanks, and they had decided that I might bring him luck, particularly when Jurek was hovering around like some hawk that seemed to have swooped down from one of the castle's million turrets. Whenever Jurek came to North

Carolina, he scrutinized every scene, every image, every inch of dialogue. But he could enchant cast and crew, win them over with tales of the illustrious guests who had visited the Vanderbilts at Biltmore House. He mentioned a quarrel Henry James and Edith Wharton had had on the castle's front lawn.

"What did they fight about, love?" Pete asked with a bitter smile. I'm sure he'd never heard of Henry James or Edith Wharton.

"They fought over books," said Kosinski. "The master had seen his own novels and Wharton's in the library. He bet Wharton all his future earnings as a novelist that not one Vanderbilt inside Biltmore House had ever perused any of their books."

"And what did they do, love? Write out a questionnaire and slip it under the door of each and every Vanderbilt?"

Jurek looked askance and sniffed at Sellers with his beak, as if that might make him disappear into dust.

"The Vanderbilts did find one reader in the mansion—their butler, who devoured every book. Henry James had won the bet, but he was appalled. He'd never heard of a butler who could read books. He left Biltmore House in a hurry."

Members of the crew whistled and clapped their hands. They couldn't get enough of Kosinski, while they kept away from Pete and his little tyrannies as much as they could. He would fall into a sudden rage, hurl his shoe at a cameraman, ask Hal Ashby—the film's director—to fire some wardrobe assistant who was giving him bad vibes, he said. But if Pete was Ivan the Terrible on- and off-camera, then Kosinski was a rogue clown. He would seduce the prettiest extras by explaining how he suffered from an incurable eye disease and had to sulk inside a closet for six hours a day so that he could practice what it was like to be blind. And it wasn't a prank: We'd open the doors of some armoire at the mansion and discover the future blind man sitting crumpled up in the dark.

Sellers was at a disadvantage here. On any other film, he would have gathered up all his comic flourish, closed his eyes, and morphed into Kosinski, but he was so involved with Mr. Chance that he couldn't creep into another man's skin. He rehearsed his lines, Hamlet-like, on the Biltmore's marble stairs, and had his revenge if Jurek happened to be around when a scene was shot. He'd lost fifty pounds after his first explosion of heart attacks in 1964, and was quite gaunt in the Pink Panther films, but he decided to play Chauncey Gardiner as a fat man. He'd usurped a little of Stan Laurel's childish voice, but without Stan's hysteria and high pitch. Chauncey Gardiner talked in a baritone that seemed underwater; as near as he was to you, he always sounded far away. And Pete's eyes lit with pleasure as he attacked Kosinski in the voice of Kosinski's own creation—Chance. He'd cut into a piece of dialogue, shake his head, and start to shiver. "I'm so sorry, Mr. K., but you're standing in my sight lines."

No matter where Jurek placed himself, it wasn't good enough.

"Gee, I just can't act with that guy around."

And he drove Kosinski off the set. But he was shrewd enough not to banish him entirely. Whole scenes had to be added or scratched, and he might need the rogue to create a new patch of dialogue.

When Mr. K. reappeared after a week of exile, Sellers would win him back in his own impersonation of Peter Sellers: part Cockney, part California, part Windsor Castle.

"Jerzy, be a good chap, Jerzy, and rewrite the scene where Eve wanks off while Chance is watching the telly."

"But there's nothing wrong with that scene," Jerzy said, stealing up to Pete like some vampire prepared to suck blood.

Pete didn't contradict Mr. K. or bother to rewrite the scene with Eve (Shirley MacLaine), but mouthed whatever madness came into his skull. It was brilliant. He was a dying man who played someone who was hardly half-alive. It wasn't only the peanut in Chauncey's pants or his addiction to the tube or the fact that he couldn't drive a car and prepare his own breakfast; like Pete, he had a strange defection in his heart and could do little more than mimic and mime; and in Mr. Chance, Pete masked his own cruel rage and rambled about in the void of a man-child who couldn't have recognized his own name.

⟞⟝

I SHARED A ROOM WITH JUREK in a cottage on Swan Street that looked as if it belonged in a fairy tale; the winding streets of Biltmore Village were paved with bloodred brick; the outer walls of each cottage were dotted with a kind of rough, pebbly skin; the roofs were made of red tile. I had to wonder if this immaculate replica of a Norman village, with its cathedral, and rectory, and tiled roofs, was the collective nightmare of the Vanderbilt clan.

I didn't see much of my roommate. He was either rutting around with some script girl or flying off to another project. And while he was away, I read another of his novels, *Cockpit*, which tells the story of Tarden, a secret agent who has left "the Service"—some phantasmagoric CIA—and wanders the world, causing mischief wherever he can. Tarden *was* Kosinski, or at least a mock-heroic version of him. The book reminded me of *Steps*, with its leap from episode to episode, but *Steps* was about real paranoia and pain, and in *Cockpit* the pain was anesthetized, so that Tarden hops about like a superhero with little at risk.

And this was the Tarden-Kosinski I saw in '79. He wasn't Pluto any longer. He had little time for the night crawlers in Harlem's Polish forest. He'd become akin to a rock star, with his birdlike profile appearing on Dick Cavett, Johnny Carson, and a hundred other talk shows. You found him in the society pages, photographed at a gala with the baroness and Mr. and Mrs. Henry Kissinger, or at a writers' conference, championing some Polish novelist in prison; it was hard to tell if Jerzy Kosinski himself belonged in *Cockpit* as one of Tarden's masks.

At the Biltmore mansion, on and off the set, Jerzy was playing Jerzy. He bullied and seduced, bullied and seduced, like Tarden up to his tricks. But the span of his wings was nowhere as great as Pete's. Pete didn't have to manipulate or woo. He understood the murderous side of his own nature. He tolerated Jurek while there were still lines to be written, but once the film wrapped, Pete went for blood.

He took his revenge by shoving Jurek right out of the story. The film ends with Mr. Chance "levitating" on the water, like some wordless wizard. And with a touch of malice, Pete had a new ending tacked onto the film; as the final credits roll, we find Peter Sellers in a series of outtakes; he's sitting on a table with his injured leg, waited to be xrayed in Benjamin Rand's own labyrinthine hospital inside his mansion.

Sellers flubs his lines and starts to laugh; and he flubs the same lines again and again. He's no longer Mr. Chance, but a comic actor, Peter Sellers, with dominion over the film and Kosinski's own characters. And he obliges us to realize that *Being There* is all about him. He's abandoned Stan Laurel's meek voice. And with his own little laughing fit, he obliterates Jerzy Kosinski and Mr. Chance.

−11−

J UREK WASN'T THE ONLY CASUALTY OF *Being There.* Sellers fired
me a few months after the film wrapped. Wires had crossed
somewhere in his skull, and I became Jerzy's accomplice. There was
no point pleading with him. He told me not to bother returning
to the Dorchester. He'd married again—his fourth and final wife,
Lynne, was a little-known actress much younger than Pete. But
whatever "nest" he tried to build with his wives, he always ended
up at his suite overlooking Hyde Park.

I'd been Sellers' slave for sixteen years, his salaried sidekick, the
straight man he needed to enhance his own cruel routines. He'd fired
me before. I kept a tiny flat on Amsterdam Avenue, knowing that I'd
be locked out of Manhattan if I ever tried to negotiate another lease.
He'd call within a month, berate himself, and beg me to return at
twice the salary. I should have told him to sod off. But I could hear a
terrible loneliness in his voice, and I'd give in, accept his lucre.

It was different now. He had his young bride, and he'd wander
with her to the Swiss Alps or Nice, flare up at customs inspectors
who had the cheek to ask him for his passport—Inspector Clouseau
should have been waved through—but he was like a walking death
mask, according to the friends I still had in his retinue. His wife had
gotten rid of whoever had been loyal to him—his bodyguard, his
chauffeur—and had become sort of a nurse who connived.

But she couldn't control Pete. He left her in Los Angeles and returned to the Dorchester in July of 1980 with whatever small retinue he still had. Pete nearly died at the Dorchester. He suffered a severe heart attack on the twenty-second of July and fell into a coma. He was carted out of the hotel and taken to a hospital, where he survived for two more days. I wasn't even allowed to attend his funeral. I received a call from some secretary, who insisted that Pete did not want Archibald Diggers' grandson at the services. And should I have the gall to arrive at Golders Green, I would be thrown out the door of the chapel. She talked as if Pete were alive and whispering in her ear. It gave me the willies.

The Pink Panther had ruined him; once he played that bumbling inspector, no comedian had the right to exist other than Peter Sellers. I'd fallen in love with George Smiley, John le Carré's fat spymaster in *Tinker, Tailor, Soldier, Spy;* Smiley was a cuckold, like Leopold Bloom, and seemed to carry Bloom's sadness about on his shoulders, but was brutal when he had to be and could run a whole gallery of secret agents. I'd begged Pete to play Smiley instead of Clouseau.

But Sellers wouldn't read the book. And when Sir Alec Guinness usurped the role and played Smiley on the BBC, it was Pete himself who began to lament. "Ian," he muttered, "you prat, you allowed that grand old lady, Alec Guinness, to get to the front of the line."

Guinness had been knighted by the queen, and Pete had become persona non grata at Buckingham Palace once he lost all his privileges with Princess Margaret. And he'd also had his first success in film with Alec Guinness, playing a numbskull in *The Ladykillers*. So Guinness was always a sore point with Pete. "He's my maiden aunt, love."

And the last conversation I ever had with Pete was over Alec Guinness. It was a few months before Pete died. He must have watched Guinness in *Tinker, Tailor* on the tube, and he rang me up and started to cry like a baby.

"I've squandered it, mate, I really have. I'm the old tit, not Sir Alec. Ask me why he *deserved* to be Smiley."

"Where are you, Pete?"

I could feel him seethe in that moment of silence. "That's not relevant, Little Ian. Ask me."

"Well, why?"

"Because his fingers are much fatter than mine—truly fat. And what you see of Smiley are his fat hands. My hands are like Popsicle sticks. All he had to do was gesture with his hands and he owned George Smiley. I would have had to hide my hands, love. They would have twitched in my pockets, and I'd have looked twitchy."

"Where are you, Pete?"

"In some wankers' hotel, a minute away from doing myself in."

I didn't believe him. He was always committing suicide on the telephone.

"Ta," he said. "I'll write you into my will."

And then he had his fatal heart attack, and after his ashes were buried in Golders Green, I did receive one letter of condolence—from Kosinski. He's the last person I would have expected to write me about Peter Sellers.

But there was little rancor in Kosinski's note, and none of his usual mischief.

> *Little Ian, I was saddened to hear of Peter's sudden death. I know how entwined you were with him. I misspoke when I called you his slave. I realize how dependent one was upon the other. And, in some perverse way, how dependent I was on him. He breathed upon my Chauncey*

*and brought him to life. Meeting Chance through him, I
also met myself. I would not have considered that possible.*

*He recognized in Chance the life and death of a neces-
sary mirror. It's Borges, I believe, who says that a man journeys as far and wide as he can, and instead of breaking new
boundaries, he discovers that in all his multiple adventures
he did nothing but mark the outline of his own face.*

> *Your brother in grief,*
> *Jerzy*

I DIDN'T SEE MUCH OF MY BROTHER IN GRIEF. His star was rising.
Not only was he a pundit on talk shows but the ex bird-boy
had also become a movie actor. In 1981, he appeared in *Reds* with
Diane Keaton and Warren Beatty; he had the role of a commissar,
Zinoviev, but he was playing himself. The commissar was Jerzy
Kosinski, with his fierce eyes and hawklike features, preying upon
poor John Reed (Warren Beatty), and overwhelming the film.

Kosinski was also a presenter at the Oscars in March of '82.
He wore a shirt with many frills and a tuxedo that smoothed the
outline of his chicken chest. But he would be dragged down in a
matter of months; his entire career as a writer began to tumble like
a meager house of cards.

In June, an article appeared in *The Village Voice* that would
haunt Kosinski for the rest of his life. Entitled "Jerzy Kosinski's Tainted Words," it damned him as a plagiarist and a fraud,
declared that *The Painted Bird* had been written in Polish and that
parts of it might even have been plagiarized. Jurek had become
a literary vampire overnight, a ghoul who stole from other writers, other books, and even vampirized his own childhood—*he* was

the tainted bird. Manhattan's favorite Polish-American novelist, an heir to Kafka and Conrad, was suddenly a pariah who could not have flourished without half a dozen ghostwriters.

Kosinski's stable of friends, including Scheherazade and the Henry Kissingers, rallied around him; articles were scribbled in his behalf; meetings were called to denounce *The Village Voice,* but he appeared on fewer and fewer talk shows, and I never saw him again at the Oscars in a ruffled shirt, like some gallant who had walked right out of the Old World.

I couldn't scan *The Painted Bird* for its authenticity, and I didn't give a crap whether little Jurek wandered through the war, hiding in one place, or ran around with a comet to keep him warm. The book was a replica of his own secret life, and the monstrosities he revealed had the sting of truth; he was exiled from his parents, whether he lived with them or not. And even if some ghost had helped guide Kosinski's hand, there was still nothing else remotely like *The Painted Bird.*

A few years after the article in the *Voice,* I listened to him on NPR. A local station in Atlanta was a far cry from Johnny Carson and the Academy Awards, but it might have been a better venue for a bird-boy in retreat. It offered him the chance to plunge right back into the maelstrom without getting hurt.

"Of course I had helpers at the beginning," he said. "How could I not? Conrad knew some English as a boy and he sailed on British vessels—his English was mixed with the language of the sea. But I didn't have captain's papers. I was a scholar and a confidence man. That's how I had always survived. My English had a jagged edge, and I didn't want my readers to bloody themselves over my books."

Then he steered the interview away from the controversy of authorship to the controversy of himself. Yes, he was Jewish, but he had been protected by priests during the war, was even an altar boy, and had had to pretend he was Catholic. "I cannot function without disguises and masks," he said. "Sometimes I wear a mask a little too long. But it's difficult to discard."

He'd married the baroness that year—1987—but talked about his first wife, Martha Will, the widow of a multimillionaire. Her friends had called him a fortune hunter. They wouldn't allow him into their clubs, certain that Martha had made him rich. But it was Martha who had bankrupted him. They went to the fanciest restaurants and hotels—the Ritz, the Connaught—and it was Jurek who had to pay the tips. He carried "a moneybag," a briefcase filled with dollar bills. Whatever royalties he would earn from his writing went inside this briefcase. He had to borrow from the doormen at 740 Park, or he couldn't have gotten through the month. Martha was an alcoholic who often blacked out. She died of a brain tumor, according to Kosinski.

The interviewer was eager to learn about Stalin's daughter, Svetlana Alliluyeva. Jurek had met her in '69 at Princeton, where she had parked herself after coming to America and where he had arrived to teach on a fellowship. "I was crazy about Lana," he said. "I mean, it wasn't a love affair. We had no sexual links. But I was addicted to her—to her eyes, the smell of her hair. We were like two lost kids in the New World. I would shiver around her, and she would hold me in her arms. 'Lana,' I would say, 'I'm so sad.' But she was the sad one, caught without her children.

"I'd just published *The Painted Bird,* and the Poles had mounted a smear campaign against me, swore I had vilified their country and all its peasants. And the Soviets were smearing Svetlana, saying she was a mental case who had abandoned her own children for a life of luxury in the West. *Luxury.* We fed on chicken salad and bruised tomatoes, Lana and I. But I kept seeing Stalin in her eyes. I had worshiped Soviet Russia's Little Father after the war. It was the

Russians who had rescued me, with their tanks and their soldiers who smelled of onions and bitter tobacco. To this day I can't go into a restaurant without ordering a dish of chopped onions.

"And she'd say, 'Jurek, why are you looking at me with your Mongolian eyes?' What could I tell her? That I was some insane groupie? That I couldn't believe I was sharing chopped onions and a chicken sandwich with Stalin's daughter? I had to hide behind a writer's wit. 'Lana,' I said, 'I'm in love with you. Let's get married.'

"And she laughed. 'Jurek, it would only lead to my third divorce. We're not suited as marriage partners. Neither of us is practical. You can't clean, and I can't cook. We would end up living on a mountain of our own garbage. But you can still be my brother for life.'

"*Her brother for life.* She moved away from Princeton and married one of Frank Lloyd Wright's apprentices. That's the last I ever heard of Lana. There was idle talk that she'd landed on the moon, and was incarcerated in some asylum. It sounds like Soviet propaganda—'*Who else but a lunatic would ever leave the motherland?*'

"But Lana was no lunatic. How could Stalin's daughter, raised on apples, onions, and the Kremlin's own soup, have thrived in the land of Snow White? She must have got lost on some American prairie and couldn't read the exit sign. I miss her. I was much less lonely when I ate chicken salad with Stalin's little redhead. She was the only real sister I ever had."

~

I MISSED LANA, TOO. Perhaps it's because Jurek was a much better storyteller when he talked about someone else's travail. I had my own troubles. I slipped into petty crime, or at least the fringes of it. I was fifty years old. My looks were going; I couldn't afford to have my teeth fixed. I became the caretaker at

a "Gestapo cellar," an S&M club that didn't seem to have a fixed
location. Nefertiti's Harbor catered to married couples. Its guests
were all anonymous: the marquis, the admiral, the duchess. But
I could have sworn that I spotted Senator Jaspers and his Scheherazade under the discreet wisdom of a black mask. They didn't
stay more than five minutes, or involve themselves with certain
regulars like the marquis or the duchess, who cried with delight
whenever a man or woman in a mask peed into a flowerpot.

Nefertiti's Harbor had its own Queen of the Night, a dominatrix named Anna Karenina, who ran the club for her best clients.
She must have been seventy years old. There were all sorts of tales
about Anna Karenina, that she had once made it with Marilyn
Monroe, and that Jack Kennedy liked to have the soles of his feet
whipped with velvet cords.

"It humbled him," she said. "And it had a medicinal purpose—it relieved the pain in his lower back."

I didn't believe or disbelieve Anna Karenina; she paid me to
listen and to keep order at the club. I never had to wear chains,
and I was never whipped.

"Ian," she liked to say, "you're immune to my charms. It's a pity
that you're not a boy who thrives on pain. Can you believe I was
once beautiful? Marilyn couldn't take her eyes off me."

I didn't find her seductive in the least. She had as much sexuality
as an animal trainer in a circus. But Anna Karenina is the one who
brought up Jerzy Kosinski.

"Ian, have you read *The Painted Bird*?"

"Yes, Anna, every page."

"I'm in the book. He modeled Ewka after me, that little string
bean with the goiter who prefers a goat to any boy or man. Ewka
broke his heart, and so did I. . . . Ian, confess. Don't I remind you
of that little string bean?"

"Yes," I told her without hesitation. I couldn't have handled my rent without Anna Karenina.

And the very next time that Nefertiti's Harbor convened, a man appeared in a mask that was an exact mold of Kosinski's face. It disturbed me because it hadn't leapt out of Pluto's forest—it was the mask of someone flaunting his own fame. The tall woman near him must have been the baroness, with her masculine features that no mask could hide. Together they seemed to rule over the séance.

I didn't dare approach them. I was the hired help who passed around the potato chips—alcohol was never served at Anna Karenina's. But Jurek approached me. He was smoking a cigarette in the space between the mold of his mouth. And for a moment it seemed that the mask itself was on fire. But it was nothing more than the practiced illusion of Nefertiti's lighting.

"Ian," he said between licks of the cigarette. "You'll have to forgive me. I asked Anna to hire you. I've been keeping up with your career."

"Jurek, I haven't seen you in ages."

"But I've seen you at least six times, dear boy. You wouldn't have noticed. I have a penchant for disguises. I followed you around."

I couldn't hide my anger. I felt humiliated, defeated by Jurek's own metaphysics.

"Did you think so little of me that you couldn't say hello?"

His pupils gleamed like black marbles in the eyeholes of his mask.

"I meant to say hello. But I was enjoying my little game too much—the pleasure of watching you."

"Like Mr. Chance. But I don't want to be part of your game, Jurek. Please spy on someone else."

"We're all tricksters," he said. "But I promise to say hello next time."

He bowed in his Mephisto mask and disappeared with the baroness.

I FELT LIKE A HAUNTED MAN. I hadn't come to terms with Jurek. He did look out for me in his own way. Perhaps I was another freak in Pluto's forest—I would never have found Nefertiti had it not been for Jurek. And so I went up to that forest in Harlem again, to the freak show of parading prostitutes. But Jurek wasn't there. And most of the freaks were gone.

I could have survived on my gigs at Nefertiti's, but I also worked the different street fairs in Manhattan. I sold secondhand books. It wasn't very profitable, because I didn't pay much attention to current tastes. I had twenty copies of *Lolita,* five of *Ulysses,* ten of *The Painted Bird.*

And once, on an autumn afternoon, Jurek wandered out of the rain and into my bazaar of books. He wasn't wearing a molded mask, but a watch cap that cut across one of his black eyebrows.

"Bravo, Ian, you're the last little soldier of literature in all of Manhattan."

"Jurek, I'm sorry. I shouldn't have been so rude at Nefertiti's."

"I was the one who was rude. I involved you in my games. . . . I've just come back from Poland. Toured the country like a lion— and a lost son. *The Painted Bird* hasn't been translated into Polish, but everyone seems to have read the book."

"Even the secret police?"

Jurek laughed. "Of course. It's a policeman's bible, full of tricks. In Cracow, in Warsaw, in Lodz, people would come in through the window wherever I spoke and carry me into the streets . . . and here I have to wonder if people will spit in my face."

"Come on," I said. "You're not really an outcast."

"How can I be while you stand in the rain with my books?"

Some customers arrived at my booth; I took my eyes off him for a moment, and the bird-boy was gone, but not for good. Jurek returned in twenty minutes wearing a sou'wester, like some fisherman adrift in Manhattan. The rain slid off his oilskin hat and coat. He was carrying a contraption that reminded me of a doctor's bag or a salesman's sample kit, but made of cardboard, or so it seemed. The rain beat on this bag with a terrifying intensity—Jurek could have held a drum in his hands.

He was weeping like a little boy under his sou'wester.

"Jurek, what's wrong?"

He reached into his sample kit and pulled out stacks of hundred-dollar bills. "I have ten thousand dollars," he said. "It's yours."

I was perplexed. My inventory of books wasn't even worth a hundred-dollar bill.

"What's wrong?"

"I want you to kill me," he said.

−12−

~

W E WENT TO A COFFEE SHOP, sat in the back, where people couldn't spy on us. It was odd. His face itself had become a mask of skin—with bumps and gnarls of flesh all over, like a great carbuncle.

"Look at Jerzy," he said. "Jerzy had to stop skiing—it's his heart. And yesterday he cracked a tooth biting into a biscuit. He'll have to live for the rest of his life on buttermilk. *Kill me.*"

"Cut it out. I won't be your angel of death."

"But you need the money. And what could be simpler? You'll sit with me. We'll talk about women. I'll take some pills, and when I get a little sleepy, you'll put a bag over my head."

"Lovely," I said. "You planned it to the letter. Why can't the baroness be your helpmate?"

"I don't want her involved in this. She'll start to cry . . . and I'll get distracted."

That lunatic began to cackle. "Mr. Chance never used your capabilities."

"You mean Peter Sellers."

"It was playing Chance that killed him, really. He could never climb out of that role. But he should have exploited your talents."

"As an assassin. But Jurek, I'm only an assassin in your dreams."

"That's not what Anya tells me. She says you're the terror of her club. Her best clients are frightened of you. . . . They want to be whipped to death by Little Ian."

"Anya shouldn't have given my secrets away."

"It doesn't matter. Your Mr. Chance should have paid you to strangle me. I deviled him on the set of *Being There.*"

I didn't want to remind Jurek that it was Sellers who had seized the film, stolen it away.

"Let's have a rehearsal," he said, "a dry run."

"Stop it!"

The baroness appeared at our table. She must have been searching everywhere for Jurek. He shouted at her.

"Why do you follow me? I'm plotting with my friend."

"You have no friends," she said.

The baroness had dark circles under her eyes. She drank from Jurek's coffee cup. He fell against her shoulder.

"Mr. Diggers, you must not encourage him. He doesn't write; he doesn't sleep. It exhausts him just to play Jerzy Kosinski."

⌐⁓

THE BARONESS WAS RIGHT. A few months later, she discovered him soaking in the tub with a plastic bag twisted around his head. The obituaries hinted at a heart condition and a suicide note—it was May of '91.

I went to Anna Karenina, searching for some sense to Kosinski. I didn't wait for the next séance of her club. I visited Anna at her tiny penthouse on the Upper East Side. Every one of her bookcases held a *matryoshka,* that mysterious Russian doll within a doll, with its labyrinthine cave where each doll had a tinier replica inside itself, like a secret hollow of pregnant dolls. Anna could feel my fascination for the *matryoshka.* And it was funny. Without the leather stuff of a dominatrix, she did have a strange, ethereal beauty in her close-cropped silver hair. She was dressed in a mourner's shawl of black lace. And she couldn't stop crying.

"Jurek loved my dolls. He said he couldn't have conceived *The Painted Bird* without them. . . . I'm his widow."

"What about the baroness?"

"A devoted clerk," said Nefertiti. "The baroness kept track of his mistresses in a little book, but Jurek was mine. He was my own little Gypsy. He would hide in the closet while I made love to other men. And after they were gone, he'd lure me into the closet and jump on me for five minutes. It was sweet. Jurek fucked like a little boy.

"And if he was despondent, so what? That's the national disease of Poland. He'd have black moods where he couldn't write for a month. . . . People call him a faker who needed other writers to write. When I first met him, he had a hard time scribbling a letter to the telephone company. That's how rotten his English was. I had to help him with it. He didn't have ghostwriters; he had baby-sitters who held his hand."

No baby-sitter from here to Mars could have scratched out the icicle-covered sentences in *The Painted Bird*. And after rereading the book for the sixth or seventh time, I realized that suicide was built into its very fabric, as if the narrator were locked into some kind of frozen grief, and had survived the war on fierce will alone. His entire life had become a chess move or chapters pasted onto *The Painted Bird*. Perhaps fate itself was a Russian doll. And Jurek's leap into the darkness was another *matryoshka*, a doll without end.

LANA, 1969

—13—

᠆

BROTHERS AND SISTERS, YOU CANNOT IMAGINE how homesick I was. I did not miss the intrigue of Moscow and calls from the premier's direct line saying how Svetlana had misbehaved again. I could not break with the *nomenklatura*. It was the curse of my red hair. I was noticed wherever I went. Citizens would bow and beg for the opportunity to kiss my hand. But I did not want to be their freckled princess. They had loved my father to madness, no matter what the Politburo said about him and his cult of personality. The *nomenklatura* was frightened to death that he might return from the grave one fine morning with his dark eyes—the *dedushka* of Moscow—and haunt them until they went screaming into their own graves. And so I lived under a kind of elegant house arrest—with a dacha that my Soviet brothers and sisters would have murdered their mothers to have as their own.

I adored our one-track railroad and the graveyard next to the station, where I longed to lie down forever—I was mortally tired in a Moscow where I was watched at every step. I had to join the Party, or my father's minions would have eaten me alive. I was put on display like a museum piece, told whom to marry, whom not to see. I disobeyed them as often as I could. After their *dedushka* died, suffering a stroke and lying in his own piss until his minions found him, his eyes roaming like a brutal animal that could no longer bark, I thought I would be free of the whole Party apparatus. I began using my mother's maiden name, Alliluyeva, but I was still *Stalina* to them, the dictator's bad little daughter. I had no peace except when I was at Zhukovka with my old nurse, who died in 1956 and left me a little orphan of thirty years.

I am a selfish girl, no less brutal than my father. I felt abandoned, betrayed by poor Alexandra Andreyevna. What I missed most were the pared apples I would find next to whatever seat I settled in. The freckled princess cannot pare an apple for herself. You see, Alexandra Andreyevna had been my nurse ever since I was born. She had a marvelous appetite for everything—food, people, books. The personages in Gogol and Gorky were as genuine to her as my own uncles and aunts. She would converse with them and expect immediate answers. They wore the same flesh as I did, and could be just as devious. I would hear her scream at Gogol's poor clerk for having lost his overcoat and berate Anna Karenina after she fell in love with Vronsky.

"Anya," she would cry, *"Vronsky isn't worth one hair on your head!"* But the problem is that she muddled the personages in *Anna Karenina* and *War and Peace,* mixed them into one big stew, and her greatest wish was to have Anna fall in love with that clumsy bear, Pierre Bezukhov. She had become a matchmaker in her old age, and was wiser than us all. Not even my father, who was a passionate reader until the end, could have equaled my nurse's love of books.

I'm curious what she would have done with *The Painted Bird.* Would she have kidnapped the mute little boy from the Polish peasants and delivered him to Saint Petersburg? But Tolstoy's counts and countesses were just as vicious as the Poles, and she might have left the little boy where he was.

It was the first book I was able to finish after I arrived in America. Brothers and sisters, you cannot imagine what it meant to have that book in my hand, to turn its pages. My father did not want me to study American literature, and there was little of it to find in Moscow—some Hemingway stories, a book or two by Dreiser, and that was half the repertoire.

"Do you want to become another herring with ideas? Study something useful, else you'll become a parasite."

And so I studied American history and social science, and my professors, normally as meek as mice, sometimes managed to smuggle a short story by Mark Twain into the class—we devoured it with tears in our eyes. It was about the Mississippi, the cruelest of rivers, brown with mud, and we all imagined what that brown river must have been like. At first my professors and classmates were suspicious of me, the freckled princess who could have been Comrade Stalin's own spy. *Bozhe moy,* I was imperious at times, with a bodyguard who accompanied me into the class.

I would dismiss him with a wave of my hand. *"Boris, if you don't leave at once, I'll scratch out your eyes and tell my father that you provoked me."*

But after Boris was gone, I did not behave like a *tsarevna.* I settled in, listened, and showed my eagerness to learn.

"Comrade Professor, we must have more American novels."

"And if the People's Police find us with such books, Comrade Stalina, what should we do?"

"Raise our hands and accompany them to the Lubyanka, where we will continue our seminar," I said, and started to laugh. From then on we had our own conspiracy in class, and like little scavengers, we looked about for American classics. We found nothing but a few brittle books with missing pages and broken spines. They were our hidden treasures. The strangest of them all was by

William Faulkner, who had not yet won the Nobel Prize, given to capitalist dogs and parasites, as my father loved to say.

It was called *The Sound and the Fury,* and we did not understand a word. But the music of the language compelled us, and we took turns reading sentences out loud. If I fell in love with America, it was through the melancholy sounds of such a book.

We discovered Faulkner's name in a forbidden encyclopedia, written by M. S. Morosov, a former prince who died in an insane asylum. Just because he was discredited, we clung to Prince Morosov's words.

> *W. Faulkner is a recluse and a drunkard who owns a mansion in Mississippi and writes about degenerates. His books are peopled with imbeciles and near imbeciles and men who are mobsters or malignant farmers such as Flem Snopes. Faulkner's women are even more degenerate than his men. They are a prime example of rural capitalism gone sour. Faulkner himself was an airman who fought on the Canadian side during the internecine War of 1914– 1918, when the capitalists set about to kill one another. Faulkner was shot down over France by a German fighter squadron and returned from the war an invalid, like E. Hemingway. At first his writing found little favor in the greedy warrens of Manhattan publishers. And when his novels were finally published, they fell upon a deaf ear.*
>
> *Faulkner could not support his family. He had to enslave himself to the hucksters of Hollywood. But he was an abysmal failure as a crass writer of scripts. He returned to Mississippi with his tail tucked between his legs and eked out a living as a hunter and a guide.*
>
> *His novels would only be of marginal interest to the*

Soviet reader, but nevertheless they do reveal the chica-
nery of rural capitalism. Faulkner writes in the so-called
southern tradition, with thick, thorny sentences encum-
bered with patch after patch of purplish prose. And yet he
has a strange power to move and disquiet the reader with
his mournful tone.

We had to decipher Prince Morosov, reach under his protective mask. He had a passion for Faulkner that would have made him an instant enemy of the people. And so in the mirror world of Soviet critics writing about the West, he had to present Faulkner as a mediocrity and a parasite. But even that did not save him. He was carted off to the asylum with his encyclopedia, which we had to read in *samizdat*, and supposedly he starved to death.

I had hoped that my stay in America would be one long feast of William Faulkner and other "degenerate writers." But with-out my class to guide me, I could not get through his impos-sible webs. And it was worse than that. I did not understand this strange American idiom, this slang of bubble gum and corrosive candy. The culture here could not enter my heart. I had settled in Princeton because I was told that the countryside would remind me of my dacha at Zhukovka. The only thing Princeton had was a tiny railroad line, with a train that was called "a dinky." This train amused me much more than the houses on my street, Stan-worth Lane. My lawyers and mentors—I had a million of them in America—had rented the house from a professor on leave, and it was in his library that I found *The Painted Bird*.

It transported me out of Princeton, and its nest of perfect little streets, into the embattled lands of Europe, where I, too, was a war orphan, though my father was still alive in '43 and '44—he had abandoned me to save the motherland. But I had felt the same terror as that little boy. I wept after reading *The Painted Bird*—not like a woman in a new land, but like the spoiled little girl who wanted her *papushka* to bounce her on his knee and smother her in kisses with that wonderful smell of tobacco.

I could barely leave my "dacha" on Stanworth Lane. I was imprisoned within its narrow walls—Svetlana Alliluyeva, the dictator's daughter, who was one more herring with ideas, had become the most famous "defector" in the world. People stared at me wherever I went. They clutched at me, begged to have my autograph. Lecture agents bombarded me with offers, said I could make half a million dollars on a single tour of college campuses, churches, and synagogues. I declined their offers. I was like my father in this way. Once, when he had gone to visit his native Georgia after the war, the townspeople had put red carpets on the roads for their *papushka*, and stood beside the carpets, waiting for him. My father could not bear it. He canceled his tour and never returned to the Caucasus.

Each morning, one of my lawyers' secretaries would bring me a mountain of mail. People in Nebraska or Kansas—good people, kind people—offered to adopt me, have me become their own daughter. I answered each letter, thanking the families of Nebraska, and signed my name—*Lana*. That's who I had become. Not Svetlana, the freckle face from Moscow, but *Lana*, the pioneer. Lana was an American name, no? I had the right to borrow it from Lana Turner, the beautiful blond witch of Hollywood films. Couldn't I be a vamp and a witch even if I did not have all the Western wiles of seduction?

But I did want to meet a man. Jerzy Kosinski, who was also a defector. He had run from the Polish People's Republic. I studied his picture on the back of *The Painted Bird*. He had all the darkness of a defector—he must have been a Jew, like my *Lyusia,*

Aleksie Kapler, the only man I had ever loved. I met him in '42, when I was sixteen and he was a filmmaker of thirty-eight, with a beautiful wife into the bargain. But we looked into each other's eyes and both of us were struck with the same lightning bolt. My own aunts dismissed my love for Lyusia as a fit of vanity, a schoolgirl's crush. But that couldn't stop me from seeing him. We had to meet furtively, like a pair of Georgian bandits on the run. He would wait for me outside my school, and I had to get rid of my watchdog, send him on some idiotic errand, while Lyusia and I sneaked off to an abandoned fairground and kissed wildly until our tongues swelled with sweet blood. We fooled no one, certainly not my father. He raged for half an hour, said he would kill me if I wouldn't give up Kapler—"a parasite who feeds on schoolgirls."

I was frightened for Lyusia's life. I swore I wouldn't ever see him again. I had my bodyguard stick to me like a leech. But it wasn't much of a maneuver. Kapler would always find me. He was reckless at a time when few men were bold and would have risked my father's wrath. I trembled each time we kissed. Kapler took me to the very walls of the Kremlin while soldiers rushed about in the middle of war. I'm grateful that my father didn't have him clubbed to death or provide him with a one-way ticket to the Lubyanka. But he had my Lyusia sent to Stalingrad as a war correspondent, hoping that Kapler might get killed by a stray bullet or a bomb. But Lyusia was even more reckless than I could have imagined—he published a letter from a certain "Lieutenant L.," which described our strolls through Moscow. My dear idiot had slipped a love letter to Stalin's daughter into the pages of *Pravda*. He was summoned back to Moscow. We went to the movies together and kissed in the dark.

But even the craziest idylls cannot last. My poor Lyusia vanished from the streets of Moscow and ended up in a labor camp . . . and seeing Jerzy Kosinski's wild eyes on a book jacket plunged me back to the war years and the sweetest moments I had ever had—both these men were cursed with wild Jewish eyes.

I wrote a letter to my band of lawyers, demanding that they find Jerzy Kosinski for Lana the *tsarevna*. I didn't expect much from my little ukase. I went back into hiding, and broke my isolation long enough to meet one of my mentors at the Nassau Inn. People whispered and pointed to me. I delivered my autograph like a dutiful daughter and disappeared after a glass of wine.

Then one morning, there was a knock on my door. Was it the postman with some poisonous letter from the KGB? No one in Princeton had my address.

"Go away," I growled. "Lana isn't at home."

This intruder of mine knocked again.

"If you're KGB," I said, "I'll scream for the Princeton police."

"Lana, let me in."

"Whore, who told you my American name?"

"I'm Jerzy Kosinski."

"And why should I believe you? What is Jerzy Kosinski doing in Princeton?"

"We're neighbors," he said with that guttural *r* of a KGB man, or a Polish exile. "I live next door."

Bozhe moy, it was like one of Krylov's fables—I read a Polski's book, dream of him, and he appears outside my door.

I undid the latch and let him in.

Pah! I couldn't even hide my disappointment. I saw a man with a weakling's narrow shoulders, and wearing a velvet suit, like one of the dandies who paraded up and down the Arbat after the war.

He started to babble in *russki*. He must have thought he was serenading Stalin's daughter in her mother tongue. His Russian was atrocious. I put a hand over his mouth.

"Please," I said, "we're not on Red Square."

I was nervous, brothers and sisters, and a little forlorn. I'd had heartbreak, brawls with my father, and several months of bliss with Lyusia, but never so strange a year as the one I had in Princeton, with a dacha and a dinky and a neighbor next door.

−14−

I COULD WIND KHRUSHCHEV AROUND MY FINGERS. I'd grown up with him. He had been one of my father's hatchet men in the Ukraine. And whenever he summoned me to the Kremlin, we would have a good cry.

"*Svetochka*," he'd say, "*you mustn't misbehave. You're a member of the Party. But you do not attend our congresses. You won't march in our parades. And when I ask you to teach at the university, you tell me that you have nothing to teach.*"

"*I'm shy, Uncle Nikita. I could not talk in front of a class.*"

He'd caress my forehead with his fat fingers. And I knew that no harm would come to me or my son and daughter while Khrushchev held the reins. But then his own disciple, Leonid Brezhnev, toppled him and brought back the cult of Stalin. Perhaps that is why Brezhnev was so harsh with me.

I was frightened every time the telephone rang. I would have let it ring until doomsday were it not for the spies that Brezhnev had stationed inside and outside my dacha—gardeners, cooks, babushkas, and other busybodies who reported back to the secret police. And so I listened to his monotonous attacks, delivered in a voice that had no inflection or sense of flavor. He never shouted like Uncle Nikita. He dreamt only of the American cars with tailfins and long obscene noses that he loved to drive

through Moscow or on deserted country roads at a catapult-
ing speed; Muscovites were frightened of Brezhnev's Buicks and
would avoid the streets whenever he passed in his cavalcade; he
was bored by everything but his cars and the Boss, as my father
had been known in Party circles. And because of this, I suffered;
Brezhnev considered me a no-account who had sullied the name
of Stalin, but I was also a magical personage, an oracle who might
lead him back to the Boss.

*"Citizen Alliluyeva, why have you forsworn your father's name?
Are you not proud to be the Boss's daughter?"*

"I am proud, Leonid Ilyich." I was the *tsarevna*, after all, and
could address the new tsar as intimately as I wished, even though
I trembled. *"But I wanted to guard my mother's memory. It is not
at the Boss's expense."*

*"But you must share your father with us, and not guard him as
a secret. The Boss had one daughter. It is your duty to write a book
about him."*

"I am not a writer, Comrade Brezhnev," I purred as a *tsarevna*
ought to purr. But it was a lie. I had written a memoir, but it
took me months to find the shape. I settled on a series of letters
to an unknown friend, scribbled in secret at my dacha during
the summer of '63. I was no Turgenev. I could not write little
polished jewels about my mother, who had killed herself when
I was six, or about the *dedushka* of Moscow, who had driven her
to suicide and mourned her for the rest of his life. My mother
could not tame the wolf; she could only give him a softer face to
wear for a little while. The wolf did not devour so many of his
countrymen while my mother was still alive. She had been strict
with me. It was *papushka* who carried me in his arms, who sang
me songs. But after my mother died, the wolf returned to the forest. If he was wifeless, then his minions would have to be wifeless

men. They could no longer bring their wives to his dacha or his apartment at the Kremlin or to the Bolshoi. He had the wife of Molotov, his most loyal minion, sent to a labor camp—but she was one of the luckier ones. Polina survived. She had been my mother's best friend.

Brothers and sisters, how could I have shown such a book to Brezhnev? He would have seized my children, sent me to live in the tundra like a convict. But when I ran off to America, I did publish *Twenty Letters to a Friend*. It caused a scandal in Moscow. I was called "the blind Kremlin princess," who had been raised in splendor and knew nothing of her own country, who had abandoned her children to become a mascot and a tool of the West. The Poliburo spread all sorts of lies: The CIA had plucked me out of an insane asylum. I was a nymphomaniac and an incurable liar. I had bartered my soul for *dollari*. I was a worthless bag of shit.

Jurek found me in this miserable state. Brezhnev wouldn't let me talk to my children more than once a twice a year. And when we did talk, they were guarded and morose. I could imagine Brezhnev's own minions hovering behind them. My son, Josef, was already a grown man. He was cold and harsh. He must have thought I was a harlot who had lain with all the fatted calves in the West. My daughter, Katya, was much more gentle with her *mamushka*. But she was equally bewildered. How would I ever explain to her and Josef that I couldn't breathe around the *nomenklatura*? I was a prisoner in one huge prison farm. Here I could breathe. But so what? I was still a freckle face, still Stalin's daughter, even with my *dollari*. And I would never find the Russian countryside near Stanworth Lane.

Jurek called me *kretinka*—"little cretin"—because my mind was sluggish in America and it took me a long, long time to gather my thoughts. But I wasn't concerned. I laughed. Kapler had called me his *kretinka,* so it was a name of love.

I had American friends. Their limousines would arrive and carry me to extravagant dinners, where I met ambassadors and their wives, who made me feel like a tamed beast in a menagerie. They fed me crackers and I performed. But they were the real menagerie. They were the ones behind a great glass wall. And I was the interloper who did not fit, *la fille maudite,* as the French ambassador might have said about some girl who had just escaped from a leper colony.

Jurek was my first foreign friend. I did not see America in his dark eyes. He could call himself a Gypsy or a Catholic with olive skin, but he was a *zhid,* like my Lyusia. And when he started telling me his baptism tales, I laughed in his face.

"My little altar boy. Shame on you, Jurek. You have as many legends as a KGB man."

"But Lana dear, it is with legends that I survived."

I could pinch his face, touch him—normal behavior in Moscow, where people are always touching. Noses and ears are the loveliest of handles. I once saw a child clutch her father's nose for half an hour on the train to Zhukovka. But here, in America, people never touch until they're under the bedcovers. *Bozhe moy,* if a woman clutches a man's nose on the streets of Princeton or at the Nassau Inn, she's both a nymphomaniac and a fortune hunter. But I couldn't help myself with Jurek. I liked to pinch his face. It didn't mean a marriage proposal. I was, he said, the sister he had never had.

"I was also a sister once," I told him. "I had two brothers, but both of them are dead."

"And what killed them, Lana dear?"

"My father's contempt. Had my mother lived, they might have

lived. She shielded them from my father and his black moods. He was crazy about me when I was a little girl. He couldn't stop kissing me. If I had ordered him to jump out the window, well, he might have jumped. But he never did one thing for my brothers. . . . Did you have a brother, Jurek?"

"No—yes, not a real brother. His name was Henryk. My father brought him home from somewhere—an elf's forest, I don't know. He had blue eyes and blond hair. He came with his own nurse. Henryk was our camouflage, our protective cover."

"To fool the Germans, eh? Show them that you weren't a band of Gypsies."

Jurek couldn't smile like most men; his lips were much too thin, and he looked like a jackal whenever he smiled.

"Lana, why do I confess such things to you?" he said, with that jackal's smile. "I never discussed Henryk with another living soul. It's your freckles. I can't resist them."

We were sitting in our usual corner at the Nassau Inn—it was a cellar aboveground called the Yankee Doodle Tap Room; Jurek told me that Paul Revere and other patriots had once sat in our corner booth during the American Revolution. I wasn't so impressed.

"Jurek, I've had enough of revolution and Yankee Doodle. Did Albert Einstein ever sit at our table?"

"He wasn't a complete imbecile, Lana dear. It's the best table in the house."

"Did he flirt with many women while he was here?"

"Thousands—no woman could resist his white mustache."

We laughed in our own dark corner, holding hands like lovers. But Jurek was too lazy to seduce me—it's more complicated than that. He was a little frightened of the *tsarevna*. He was in awe of Stalin. The Russians had saved his skin. His heroes weren't Patton and Eisenhower, but ordinary Russian soldiers, as I could tell in *The Painted Bird*. The Red Army had captured and slaughtered rebellious Kalmuks, who were even more dreadful than the Germans. The Kalmuks would wipe out entire Polish villages, raping women and children, robbing the eyes of old men, until the Red Army broke their necks.

And for a little boy liberated by Stalin and growing up in a satellite country ruled by Stalin, what else could he have imagined? Stalin was his little father, a god who had his own earthly paradise called the Kremlin. America was some afterthought, a secondary dream, a tiger he didn't have to chase by the tail. And when my father died, Jurek must have mourned him as much as I ever did. It made him even more delirious over Moscow. He saw his future in my father's land, as a pioneer in Russia's great social laboratory. All of us believed in some craziness like that. He first visited Russia in 1951, as a student. Brothers and sisters, what could the pioneer have found in Moscow and the provinces? A bureaucracy even more crippling than the one in Poland. Fat commissars in fast cars. A morbid fear of foreigners. A grayness that was close to gangrene. From that point on, he turned his attention to the United States.

A pioneer in a land of pioneers. What could be better? But Jurek's face was as sad as mine. We couldn't find our own hearts in this heartland. We were two of Stalin's children, laughing as hard as we could in a corner of the Yankee Doodle. I'd already had whiskey sours and white wine. But Jurek couldn't drink wine. It was poison, he said. He drank buttermilk. And I was nibbling on a monstrous piece of strawberry shortcake, which was as close as I could ever get to a charlotte russe. We occupied what Jurek liked to call "the conspirator's table," since it was in the darkest and deepest part of the taproom, where not a soul could recognize me. He was a genius at finding hidden nooks and crannies. We were, he said, the Hole-in-the-Wall Gang—outlaws with allegiance to nothing and no one.

"Lana dear, let's rob a bank. The guards in Princeton don't even bother to wear a gun. And they can't arrest you. You're too much of a prize in the propaganda war."

"But why go through all the bother? If you want a Buick, like Brezhnev, I'll buy you one. It's much, much easier to write a check. My lawyers say I have enough *dollari* to choke a hundred horses."

Whiskey sours and shortcake must have been a potent cocktail. My head was about to fall off. But I wasn't blind. Jurek's Gypsy-Jewish eyes smoldered in the dark. I'd upset my darling bank robber.

"It's not the same thing. We won't wear masks . . . or carry toy guns. The tellers will ask for your autograph while they hand us the bank's money. Lana, you'll be on the cover of *Time*."

Now I was the one who bristled. I grabbed his nose, but not with affection. I pinched it as hard as I could. "We are outcasts, my little Polish brother, in the land of strawberry shortcake. I dream of literature and wine, and all you can think about is the cover of *Time* magazine. But I love you, and if you wish to become a bank robber, I will join your Hole-in-the-Wall Gang . . . but no violence, with or without toy guns. And we must not frighten the tellers. I do not wish them to suffer heart attacks—I will not go to jail with a bad conscience."

"Lana, please," he said, "you are hurting my nose."

I pinched it one last time.

"Well, bank robber, when do we begin? But I warn you. I will donate my share of the loot to a charity that fights tuberculosis."

He smiled like a jackal. "If we give away what we steal, then it is not a robbery, but a bazaar. Besides, this isn't Moscow, Lana. There's no more tuberculosis in America. Tuberculosis has been wiped out."

"Pah," I said. "A country without tuberculosis does not have much of a soul."

I could no longer find his face. He shrank into the dark like some local Dracula. And then he started to laugh and cry at the same time, and he emerged from the shadows without his jackal's grin.

"Lana, you're impossible. You'll be the Kremlin princess until the day you die."

"I suppose so. That is my sad fate."

And both of us started to laugh and cry, until the noise bounced off the walls and brought a little bedlam to the Yankee Doodle. *Bozhe moy,* now we no longer had a place to hide.

− 15 −

WHAT DID HE DO ALL DAY? He didn't write, didn't teach, even though he was an honored lecturer, the genius who had written *The Painted Bird*. We never chatted on the phone, never conspired to meet at his own dacha, which was less than a hundred yards from my house. He was always at the Nassau Inn, where he seemed to hold court with students or professors and townspeople, his back hunched over as he whispered and intrigued. But when I arrived in my babushka and dark glasses, he would part company with the others and come over to our corner booth.

And that's how my day would begin. We were both terrible paranoiacs. I was convinced that the KGB had spiked the salads I shared with Jurek, and was plotting to kidnap me right out of the Yankee Doodle. And Jurek felt he was a marked man. The Polish secret police would never forgive him for *The Painted Bird*.

I had acquired a foul mouth in America. Jurek said I cursed like a stevedore. I considered that a compliment.

"I piss on the Polish secret police. Those *govnyuki*"—shit-heads—"should congratulate you. You've put Poland back on the map with your book."

And now he decided to play Hamlet at the Nassau Inn. "You don't understand," he said, clutching his scalp of curly hair that reminded me of Harpo Marx. "I was one of them."

"*Govnyuk,* I don't believe you."

"But it's true. I was a swan for them while I was still in high school."

"Swan," I said. "What swan?"

"A stool pigeon."

"Jurek, I can imagine you as a mass murderer, a bigamist, a charlatan, but not a stool pigeon."

"But I was arrested, Lana—after a prank. I was always doing pranks. I telephoned people, pretending to be a minor official in some ministry, told them they would have to move to another town, and that they had twenty-four hours to pack."

"Couldn't they tell it was a joke? How many people listened to you?"

"Practically all of them," he said. "That was Poland in 1950. The telephone was God to them. And God never lied. But I miscalculated. One of the women I telephoned was a member of *my* ministry. I was arrested, put in an isolation ward. My captors conducted their interrogation with all the clichés of a Polish cop—lamp in my eyes, a fist in my face. I confessed in five minutes. And then the Polish Gestapo arrived, the UB. The other cops were frightened. I don't think the UB had ever been on their premises before. The secret police took me out of my cell, shared a cigarette with me, washed my bloody face with a clean handkerchief. These men didn't disapprove of what I had done. They called my telephone games a clever trick. They asked if I would work for them. Their neckties were made of silk. That's what I noticed first. And their cuffs weren't frayed like the other cops.

"They said I didn't have to spy on my family or friends. I should just write things down in a notebook. What things? I asked. Anything that entered my mind, they said. It was enough for them that I kept a notebook. The UB would pay me once a month."

"In rubles, dollars, or zlotys?" I asked, like a member of the KGB.

"Dollars," he said. "No other currency mattered."

"And what did you write in your golden notebook?"

"Exactly what they wanted. I spied on everyone—my father, my fellow students."

"Jurek, you're not a *govnyuk*. You're a snake."

"Ah, but your kind of snake, Lana. An intelligent, pragmatic snake. I manufactured conversations; I lied with a little twist. To accuse someone of slight treason is not to accuse them at all. No one was ever arrested from the material in my notebooks. An outburst, a temper tantrum, an ambiguous word—Lana, I could ride on my writings for six years. And the UB helped smuggle me into Mother Russia, forged whatever documents I needed. They let me have one of their own beaver hats. I came to Moscow like a Polish commissar."

"Jurek," I said, gulping wine and buttermilk. "I disown you. Wherever I walk, you must walk on the other side of the street."

That was the first time we ever kissed. He reached over while I reprimanded him and took hold of my mouth. I waited until his lizard's tongue vanished into the middle of his face.

"*Skopetz,*" I said, meaning a castrated man. "I did not give you permission to kiss me."

"Lana dear, if I had to wait for permission to kiss a Soviet princess, I would have to live two thousand years."

"Twice two thousand," I said, "before I would grant you a second kiss. But tell me more about your adventures with the UB."

"There were no adventures. I took notes in Moscow, pretended to interview people, traveled on the train, had one or two romances, and returned to Lodz in my beaver hat."

I did not want this *skopetz* to see my jealous nature.

"Comrade Kosinksi of the Polish secret service, consider me your case officer. Did you acquire a mistress in Moscow or Leningrad, or in the Ukraine, a married woman who was bored to death with a husband who drank himself into blindness every night?"

"No, dear," said the *skopetz.* "I met a young student from Odessa on the train."

"A little Jewess?"

Bozhe moy, I was beginning to sound like my father! That's what jealousy will do.

"Her name was Mashenka. And she—"

"Comrade, I wish not to hear about it."

"But she had your looks, Lana. She was a freckle face with hair that flamed in the sun."

"Pah," I said. "Now he talks in poetry. I do not wish to have the details, Jurisha. What did your brothers in the UB say after they read your Russian notebook?"

"They said I was a born *sphion.* I wrote reports . . . about student unrest, loyalty to the regime. That was my beginning as a novelist—lies, lies, lies. And they decided to transport their new 'product' to America and test him there. It wasn't so easy to accomplish. I required an American university to sponsor my research. They had to troll in foreign waters. And when they couldn't find enough Polish professors to support my documents, the UB had me invent professors of my own. It was a brilliant strategy. They supplied the official stamps and letterheads. I was very modest about myself, outlining all my weaknesses. And it worked. But I'm not a fool. I couldn't afford to be discovered in America as a Polish spy. I disowned my masters, fed them nothing. And in all fairness, they left me alone . . . until *The Painted Bird.*"

"But the UB should have rejoiced. You were their creation."

"That is the heart of the problem. Now they are taking the heat."

I wrinkled my nose. "I am not familiar with such an expression—*taking heat*. What does it mean?"

"Their feet are caught in the fire. They must have considered me their mole in America, someone who could lie at rest until summoned back into service. But their mole had played a trick. His notebook was now a novel that turned their own countrymen into devils. And so they have spread all sorts of lies about Jerzy Kosinski, that he is a Jew. . . ."

"But you are a Jew, Jurisha."

"Lana, listen, please. That's not the point of their smear campaign. They're the ones who are the devils. They congratulate the book's style and wealth of detail but insist that an ungrateful *zhid* like myself does not have the right to accuse Polish peasants who saved his life and the lives of his family."

"Jurek, you told me yourself, a few nights ago, that you did hide out during the war, that your father had enough cash to buy you and your mother a whole new Catholic identity. . . ."

"But that is our secret, Lana—I could not lie to Stalin's daughter. And I love your funny little nose and your red hair."

"My nose isn't funny. And I do not want to be told secrets just because I am Stalin's daughter. Move to another table, Jurisha, or I will scream."

"Scream your head off," he said as he slid away from me and disappeared into the darkness of the Yankee Doodle.

I missed him the moment he was gone. I didn't feel alive until I could dream of tearing Jurisha's eyes out. But I couldn't seem to find him. He wasn't holding court at the Nassau Inn the next day or the day after that. And when I knocked on the door of his dacha, no one answered my knocks. I scratched a note with my favorite green pencil—my father was fond of green pencils—and folded it under Jurisha's door.

Where the devil are you, govnyuk?

But he had the gall not to answer my note. I seethed with anger and resentment. I was swollen with bile. I took my green pencil, crossed him out of my life, and went looking for him at the Nassau Inn. There wasn't a sign of my black-haired Harpo. No one, not even my father, the rudest man alive, had ever been so rude to me.

I put on lipstick and painted my eyes like Lana Turner, and then I ran across Nassau Street, into the maze of Princeton University. I was frightened of so many brick and stone buildings—it was a little Kremlin without the high walls.

I did not have Jurisha's address at the university. I had to ask and ask, twist like a dervish, until I found the building where he kept an office. I went up to a secretary and said, "It's urgent. Life-and-death. I must speak with the *maître.*"

She did not recognize Svetlana, even without the babushka. And this was the first time I had needed my new celebrity.

"I am Stalin's daughter," I said.

It made no impression. The clerks here must be imbeciles.

"But are you related to him, ma'am?"

"Yes. I'm his wife."

Now I understood how potent matrimony was in America. This same clerk was suddenly solicitous. She accompanied me to Jurek's classroom. I knocked on the door and marched in like a prima ballerina with freckles. I did not recognize him. He wore a cashmere jacket that broadened his shoulders, a brutal white shirt, and a necktie with blinding colors. His students were sitting around a long table and never took their eyes off the *maître.*

"Lana, what's wrong?" he asked, without his jackal's grin. "I'm in the middle of a class."

"Come outside, Jurisha. The class can wait."

What choice did he have? He bowed to his students like one of my father's Russian generals and stepped outside into the hall.

"Jurek, you must not abandon me again. I am a creature of habits. You disappear and never answer my notes."

"But I did not read your notes. I was in Manhattan, and I had to run to my class from the train station."

"Then how much would it have cost to tell me your plans? Is this how you treat the only other living member of the Hole-in-the-Wall Gang?"

He grabbed my hand and kissed it. I wasn't pleased. My hands are not beautiful.

"I was remiss," he said. "It will not happen again. Does Princess Lana give her subject permission to teach his class?"

"No," I said. "Not yet. You could dismiss your students and have buttermilk with me at the Nassau Inn."

He bowed—I did not like such ceremony from him.

"As Her Highness commands," he said.

He spent five more minutes with his students and then we escaped from his little Kremlin and returned to our dark corner at the Nassau Inn, my heart beating to its own silly music.

— 16 —

⟶

IF ONE OR TWO MEN LOVED ME, it wasn't because of my Lana Turner legs. I was pretty in the right places, but no matter how often we kissed or fumbled with our hands, Jurek never invited me into his bed. I was the dictator's daughter. And he couldn't glide above the ghost of my father. But that doesn't mean we were not lovers in every other way.

I sat with him through his bouts of depression, held him in my arms, serenaded him with songs my nurse had taught me. He had won a prize for his second novel, but the prize did not console him; it darkened his mood. I had no love for this novel called *Steps*. It was a heartless book. I could feel Jurek on every page. It was his own portrait of the artist as an invisible man. But for me, the novel was a masquerade, a disguise he wore to prevent himself from screaming. I wanted to hear the screams.

"Lana, the UB trained me too well."

"Idiot, they didn't train you at all. You scribbled nonsense for them and they lapped it up. That's how it is with all secret services."

"But the problem is that I'm still a secret service man. I lie even while I speak the truth. And I cover my traces with yet another trace. I'm like that guy in Gogol's story who has lost his nose and keeps running after the little monster."

"Jurisha, you have a beautiful nose, and it will never leave your face."

"But it isn't *my* nose, Lana dear. I'm a fraud. I cannot write my own novels without a helper."

"Who is she? I'll tear her eyes out."

"Yes," he said, laughing amid all his gloom. "And then Gogol's nose will take its revenge on the two of us."

And now we had a third party in our romance: Nikolai's Nose. We did not have to put it in a box. It sat with us, palpable in our own minds.

"Jurek, take us somewhere. The Nose is sick and tired of the Nassau Inn."

"But where would you like to go, *lapushka*?"

"When I was a little girl locked inside the Kremlin, I would listen to people talk of Atlantic City, with its boardwalks and Al Capone—it was the secret capital of the world."

"Lana, Capone ruled Chicago, not Atlantic City. It's a dump, a ruin that still stands. But if you blow on it hard enough, all of Atlantic City will come tumbling down."

"Good. We will blow on Atlantic City, and see what happens— how much will it cost for the three of us to take a cab?"

I should have been suspicious of his jackal's smile. If I wanted Atlantic City, he said, I would have to protect myself against the ocean breeze. So I returned to the Nassau Inn wearing my winter cape, but there was no Kosinski, not his hide nor his hair. And then a blue Buick, the kind that Brezhnev would have driven, honked at me. A chauffeur stepped out of the car in a gray uniform with burgundy-colored boots and a cap that hid his eyes.

I was furious. "You mock me, my dear. I'm not your toy poodle."

"No," he said, "you're the *tsarevna*. And you have to ride to Atlantic City with all the pomp and circumstance of your position."

"Like Cinderella in her pumpkin coach. And don't forget—her chauffeur was a rat."

"Indulge me, Lana. Get in . . . with Nikolai."

"Stop playing games. There is no Nikolai. I do not wish to travel with a phantom nose on my seat."

But I could not dethrone my chauffeur. He turned his fist into a *marionetka* and pretended to speak through the little hole he had made with his fingers.

"*Svetlana Alliluyeva, Nikolai's Nose at your service. I knew your father well. I was his favorite character. Do you remember how he would recite my journeys across Petersburg to you before you went to sleep?*"

"It's a lie," I said. "Papa never . . ."

And then I started to laugh. "You win, you win." And I plunged into Brezhnev's Buick with Nikolai's Nose in my arms.

⌒

I T WAS A MONSTROUS TOWN, with buildings that reminded me of the "white layer cakes" that rose across Moscow in the '30s, thanks to my father and his team of architects. Molotov, who did not have a drop of imagination, must have designed those white layer cakes, which were like stupid pieces in a proletarian fairy tale. Atlantic City wasn't a proletarian garden, I know, but it had the same monumental monotony. Some of its layer cakes were white, and some were redbrick, but they held the whole skyline hostage to their bewildering presence. Nothing else seemed to live or move. The men and women I saw on South Indiana Street could have been mechanical ants.

Jurek didn't even have to park his car. He gave his keys to the concierge at the Claridge. And the two of us made quite a stir. Grande dames didn't walk under the Claridge's canopy with their chauffeurs, who were supposed to wait in the garage or have a bite to eat in one of the Claridge's back rooms.

I was Russian, after all, even if I modeled myself on Lana Turner. And I didn't trust any of the matrons with my babushka or winter cape—matrons in Moscow were known to steal and covet capes and scarves for themselves. We went through the lobby arm in arm. People might not have recognized me—my nose is too short and I do not have a spectacular profile—but they whispered and pointed at us with a rudeness that would have earned them a slap in the face in my old country.

"Chauffeur, you must tell them not to stare. It's impolite."

"Lana, they worship you. They have never seen a Russian princess before."

"But their *mamushkas* should teach them manners," I said.

"Their *mamushkas* would stare at you in the same way."

"Then perhaps we should dine at another hotel."

He ignored my last remark, and one of the Claridge's lackeys escorted us into a dining room that was as large as a Soviet football field. I expected the Dynamos to arrive in their winter jerseys and make us shiver with their mastery over the ball. But there were no footballers at the Claridge—just an army of waiters and busboys to serve a wild and noisy scattering of dinner guests. The men smoked cigarettes, the women wore mascara masks, and they could not believe their eyes when they saw a chauffeur in burgundy-colored boots escort me to one of the oak tables, move his chair next to mine, summon the waiters, and demand a bottle of the Claridge's best champagne.

These barbarians gawked at us through the entire meal. I loved every moment of it. Brothers and sisters, I was having the time of my life. Jurek spoke to the waiters in French, bolted into the kitchen to confer with the chef, and had the busboys prepare a place setting for Nikolai.

"Jurek dear, it's better than a name-day party. You are the sweetest, kindest boy, and also a devil—you know in your heart what can entertain me and quicken my blood."

The men buried their noses in the wine list, but the mascaraed women were much bolder and asked me to sign their menus.

"Your Highness," one of them said, "I think it's the height of culture to have dinner with your chauffeur at the Claridge. What's his name?"

"Oh, I couldn't bother with names. I give them numbers. This is Chauffeur Number Five."

I was feeling giddy and perverse—now I knew what it was to be inside Jurisha's head, swarming with crazy contradictions.

A second or third woman asked about Nikolai's place setting. I couldn't confess that we had a personage from one of Gogol's stories at our table. She might have gotten suspicious about a wandering nose, and I wouldn't divulge my love of Russian literature to a restaurant full of barbarians.

"A tragedy," I said, patting my eyes with an enormous napkin. "Our dead son—Nikolai. He drowned at my lake near Carlsbad. We always leave a setting for him wherever we go."

They were astonished. Their mascara began to melt into their eyes—that's how much I had heated them up with my tale.

"Your Highness, you had a child with Chauffeur Number Five?"

They swarmed to our table, bringing their own chairs and beckoning their husbands after a while. We finished nine magnums of Veuve Clicquot. They were all in love with Chauffeur Number Five. But the cleverest of them, a woman whose mascara did not run, pressed her flute of champagne against her cheek, looked into my drowsy, drunken eyes, and said, "Say, aren't you Svetlana what-yer-call-it? The dead dictator's daughter?"

It was Jurek's training as a liar that rescued me.

"Her Highness likes to pose as Lana. It makes it easier for us to travel."

All my giddiness was gone. It was not so amusing after all to trick our fellow diners at the Claridge. Perhaps we were the barbarians, Jurisha and I. And I was no longer amused by Nikolai's Nose.

Jurek could sense my displeasure. He stood up and bowed.

"Her Highness is tired," he said. "She's still in mourning. She misses our son."

The others left our table. It was cluttered with debris.

"Jurisha, I would like to go now."

He snapped his fingers at a waiter and took out a credit card. I covered the card with my own freckled hand.

"Darling," I said with a bittersweet smile, darker than the darkest Russian chocolate. "What will the Claridge think? We can't have my chauffeur pay the bill."

It meant nothing, two thousand *dollari*. I was an author, no? With royalties that my bankers piled into six accounts. I could have asked for a telephone, the way Lana Turner would have done, and bought Jurek another Buick without leaving my chair. I was now a *kapitalistka*, not so much a princess.

I got up from the table without Nikolai's Nose. I left him there. I didn't want to play with invisible marionettes. My father always had Gogol at his bedside ever since I could remember. Gogol understood Russia's madness, our mania for titles, our fear of bureaucrats, so that a nose could acquire a title of its own and become another fearsome bureaucrat. But I had to rid myself of my father's ghost, or I myself would become a phantom without the semblance of a home.

— 17 —

Bozhe moy, I HAD GOGOL IN MY BLOOD. I couldn't break away from Nikolai's Nose. If I shut my eyes, I could see it run on Palmer Square. But the nose wasn't always Nikolai's. Sometimes it was my father's nose, with its wide nostrils and thick black nostril hair. At other times it was unrecognizable, except for the reddish braids that surrounded it, like an obscene sandwich. The braids were mine.

I would get up like a bolt in the middle of the night and grasp my face, needing some certainty that my nose was secure. This was Princeton, not Saint Petersburg, and I hadn't landed inside one of Gogol's stories—not yet. But it's hard to explain why I couldn't stop crying. I'd had such epic battles with my father, where hate and anger would build for months and months like a bitter, hardening wound, that I hadn't really mourned him—he'd died like a dog in his own dacha, covered in sweat and piss, and my first impulse upon seeing the rage and fear in his wolf's yellow eyes had been to make a fist. I wanted to beat him until his eyes shrank inside his skull and his face was swollen and blue.

He'd had a mistress during the last eighteen years of his life, a "housekeeper" named Valechka, who traveled with him wherever he went. She was a kind, stupid girl with a pug nose and a child's melodious voice. But Valechka, who had catered to his every whim, wasn't allowed to care for Papa while he lay dying. She was discarded by the Politburo like a rag doll. I had been jealous and petulant about her closeness to my father, though I did like her gentle ways with him, her soft seduction. She was illiterate—and I always imagined that my father read Gogol to Valechka, especially "The Nose."

More than once I'd catch her in a sort of pantomime, where she would "unscrew" my father's nose and run with it in the fields behind his dacha at Kuntsevo. How happy she was to be the possessor of my father's nose. He had often told me that books were his only life, that he had become the Soviet tsar by default, a wolf who didn't want to be eaten by other wolfs.

"*Housekeeper,*" he'd say—he liked to think of me as his housekeeper when I was his one and only obedient little girl— "*Housekeeper, I read and learn every day of my life. My own comrades do not want to lend me their books. I had my spies get to the bottom of their grumbling. They say Stalin cannot return a book without grease stains on every other page. But doesn't that grease prove that Stalin devours a book, and aren't his thumbprints a sign of his seriousness?*"

I hadn't been "Setanka" the housekeeper in a long, long time. He always had his little joke when I was a child. He would turn me into *Setanka*, the little tsar of Moscow, and Papa would play the tsar's most obedient servant, Secretary Number One. He would grovel in front of me and his minions.

"*Setanka, your wish is my command.*"

And I would fill up with pretended rage. "*Setanka says that Secretary Number One hasn't shined his shoes. His mustache is filled with crumbs. His fingernails are filthy. All of Setanka's secretaries should be ashamed of themselves.*"

Papa would shiver and laugh and shine his shoes—he always

seemed to have such a good time with his *Setanka*. No one else would have dared scold the Boss or criticize him. And how clever I was as a little girl! Brothers and sisters, I was not drunk with power. I could always tell by the color of his wolf's eyes whether he wanted to play with his *Setanka* or not. If the wolf's eyes went from bright yellow to a dull brown, the little tsar of Moscow would suddenly grow meek as a mouse.

But there was always a price to pay. *Setanka* had become an addiction. The games ended with the beginning of the war. He would scribble letters to me in his green pencil and sign them, *Josef the Peasant,* or *Your Loving Papa, Secretary Number One.* But I couldn't rage in front of his minions anymore. I couldn't command him, order him about, or even comment on the crumbs in his mustache. I hardly ever saw him, and when I did, that familiar bright yellow had fled from his eyes.

I never grew out of my addiction—not completely. I am still *Setanka,* Josef Stalin's ungrown daughter, who was eager to play, play, play. And it was my misfortune in America that Jurek revived this addiction and made it worse. I was drawn to him and his maddening games. He was my own particular devil, wearing the guise of a secret brother. I had to repeat again and again the story of *Setanka*. He would listen in ecstasy, his ears sprouting devilish points.

"Lana, don't lie. Did your father really shiver in his shoes?"

"Boots," I said. "The Boss wore boots most of the time."

A peculiar look crept into Jurek's eyes. He was the novelist now, taking notes with the green pencil inside his head, and I worried that I might become a personage in his next novel. But I couldn't help myself. I was addicted to him. And I was drawn deeper into his games.

We fed each other's paranoia, and we both felt like lambs being led to the slaughterhouse. We were at the mercy of *some* secret service—call it the KGB. The dacha on Stanworth hadn't been rented in my name. But it was clear to most townspeople who the hermit in the head scarf was. Tellers at the bank touched my hand. Princeton professors stopped me in the street. Yet Moscow swore I was a demented witch who was locked up in an insane asylum. And my devil with his curly hair reasoned that it would not have been difficult for the KGB to kidnap *Setanka* and lock her up in a real asylum. So we had to be careful.

Jurek now wore disguises at the Nassau Inn—a mustache and beard that made him look like a sinister Buffalo Bill, or else his chauffeur's cap and boots.

"Darling, it's ridiculous. You cannot pretend to be a stranger—everybody knows you at the Yankee Doodle."

But he wouldn't listen; he said it was no longer safe to meet at the Nassau Inn. I panicked—where else did I have to go? I had an ice-cream parlor on Nassau Street, a bank on Palmer Square, and a dark corner in a taproom as the three vital points of my existence, except for my library and an occasional picnic with my American friends. But Jurek insisted that we meet in Manhattan from now on.

"It's imperative," he said. "It's vital . . . and you must not tell a living soul, Lana, or you will compromise our mission."

And so I took the dinky that waited at Princeton's little depot like a private car, maneuvered in my babushka and dark glasses, and ended in Manhattan—Moscow had a much bigger crush of people, but the crowds at Pennsylvania Station frightened me because I could not follow the logic of their movements; they milled around like cattle in the midst of a mindless stampede, and I was sucked into their flow. I could not find Kosinski. I

clutched my handbag and ended up on an escalator that spat me
out into the street.

Like a child, I called out for Secretary Number One, but my
poor *papushka* didn't come. I marched under a mountain of
walls that could have swallowed up Moscow's white layer cakes.
I couldn't stand to look up into the teeth of such high crevices.
Moscow was round and overripe, with her winding streetcars,
her embankments, her population of domes that could have been
born in the dream of a drunken tsar. But Manhattan had no such
roundness—I saw the jagged lines and steep pockets of an endless ziggurat. Angels would have grown dizzy here and toppled
off the roofs.

Chorti, I whispered to myself. I had come to a devils' paradise.

One of these Manhattan devils stood behind me. He was in a
military uniform with silver braids and medals and a forage cap.
Bozhe moy, I did not recognize him until he removed the cap and
revealed his curly hair.

"Congratulations, *govnyuk.* You would scare away the Cheka
with such a disguise. Are you a general from some lost Arabian
legion? I have never seen so many different colors and ribbons on
a single uniform. Did you just step off Noah's ark? Why didn't
you meet me at Pennsylvania Station?"

"Lana, I haven't left your side. I was on the dinky with you."

"Impossible," I said. "I would . . ."

But that devil could have been sitting beside me. I struck him
in the chest with my handbag.

"Rainbow Room," I said. "It is in Rockefeller's Center. You
will take me there, please."

I had puzzled the devil, mystified him. "And what will you
find at your little tourist mecca?"

"Tourists," I said. "Khrushchev visited Rockefeller's Center with President Eisenhower. He told me, 'Svetochka, you must visit Rainbow Room. It is the only place in Manhattan that doesn't make me homesick. You sit in the sky with the angels, and it's *almost* Moscow.'"

"Lana, I'm not a magician. You have to book the Rainbow Room a month in advance."

"But you're a general, Jurek. You'll tell them that the dictator's daughter is following Uncle Nikita's footsteps and wishes to shake hands with an angel in the tourist mecca."

I T WAS MOSCOW IN MANHATTAN, even if Rockefeller's Center didn't have the warmth and savage wonder of a Russian nightclub, where the worst enemies could cry in one another's arms, where someone's wife could dance with a hundred men and her husband would see this as an honor to himself, where politicians could scheme in the open with oil tycoons, where bundles of *dollari* would pass from hand to hand, where gamblers gambled and generals brought their mistresses to be ogled by anyone in a clean shirt. Nightclubs were holy places, "cathedrals" where no one could be punished or harmed.

The Rainbow Room didn't have such a burden. It wasn't where a whole society mingled. It was never raucous. Women did not clutch their husbands' noses out of anger, love, or spite; men didn't roam from table to table, looking for other men's wives. There was a calm that must have captivated Khrushchev; a kind of soft musical hum that could have been the whisper of angels—did that sound come from the chandeliers or the diners themselves?

It was like sitting in an enormous eagle's nest with silvered walls and all of Manhattan below us; the city wasn't a ziggurat with jagged lines from our eagle's nest; the tallest buildings, with their own slight sway, had a silent hum—I did not see any angels nesting there. But I felt their presence, and it's this that must have excited Uncle Nikita.

"*Svetochka,*" he had said, gripping my arms with his fat fingers, "*there are angels in the attics at Rockefeller's Center.*"

But it was Jurek who scattered the angels and broke the calm. He could not sit still. He introduced himself at other tables as General Gogol, my military aide.

"I live my life for Lana," he said. "I have to protect her from foreign agents. The Kremlin would love to have her back. It has made a pact with other governments and their provocateurs to steal her off the street."

"But aren't you yourself Russian, General Gogol?" asked a lady doctor from Iowa who was in Manhattan for the first time.

"Yes," he said, "but we are the *rasputniki,* dissidents inside and outside the Soviet Union who have formed our own secret empire, a parallel government that disrupts Moscow wherever it can—we have chess masters and military men within our ranks, and we are dedicated to reviving the Russian monarchy, with Stalin's daughter as the new tsarina."

I sat there, a freckle face who couldn't stop blushing. A *rasputnik* in Russian was a lecher and a lout. And Jurek would have his *rasputniki* rule the world, with poor Lana on the throne. I was furious with him.

"General Gogol," I shouted, "we must leave right this minute."

He was so busy finding converts for his fable that he did not have much time for the fable's queen.

"Gogol, I command you."

His back bristled, and for a moment his uniform lost its perfect line.

"Majesty," he said, turning on his heels so that I could get a glimpse of his rage. I was ruining the concoction he had spun. The *rasputniki* were realer to him than a lonely redhead who would have to find her way back to Princeton Junction.

"Majesty, enjoy your dinner. I have to plead our cause."

I walked to the cloakroom and retrieved my winter cape. He followed me out to the elevators in his forage cap. His neck was pulsing under the collar of his tunic. For a moment I thought he would slap my face. I smiled. It was very cruel of me.

"Gogol darling, would you disfigure your own queen?"

My remark must have rescued him from his own ridiculous fable. Now he was able to laugh at himself.

"Gogol apologizes. Your general was carried away."

He kissed my hand in the elevator and wouldn't allow me to ride back to Princeton on the train.

"Lana, the dinky doesn't run late at night. You could be stranded at the station . . . please."

We took a cab to the garage where his Buick was parked. And when I wanted to sit up front with him, he started to cry.

"Please—it will be a form of punishment."

"Jurek, I won't be your punisher."

But I was tired and let him have his way; I played the tsarina until we arrived at my dacha behind Nassau Street.

He was still sobbing. "Lana, say that you forgive me."

I held him by the nose and caressed his face with my free hand.

"I forgive you, darling."

Then I ran out of Brezhnev's car. Perhaps it was reckless of me to break away from my one foreign friend in this land of Yankee Doodle. But I did not have a choice. I had to cut off the heart of my own addiction, or I would have ended up in a madhouse. I was prone to Jerzy Kosinski, just as my father was prone to *Boris Godunov*, an opera that could have killed him.

He would take me with him to the Bolshoi, the Boss and his little freckled *tsarevna* in their private box, with all his bodyguards in unbearable blue suits. And what was the opera about? A fake tsarevitch, Dmitri the Pretender, who wants to steal the crown away from Boris Godunov—and poor Boris, who had the real tsarevitch murdered, lives in a trance while the Pretender gains more and more control, and dies broken with remorse. And the people welcome their new tsar in abject silence.

Bozhe moy, this was not an opera for a Soviet tsar to share with his people. It questioned who he was and how he came to be. But he went back to the Bolshoi again and again, and would watch *Boris* with tears in his eyes. His minions at the opera were confused. Was he crying for Boris, or the Pretender, or himself? They kissed my hand and looked for answers in my eyes.

I knew their meek, miserable ways. They worried what would happen to them if my father fell? Why did he encourage rebellion, attend an opera about a false tsarevitch? Was the Boss losing his mind? He was addicted to *Boris Godunov*, had let the opera crawl under his skin, but the moment Hitler was on the march and rumbles could be heard in Moscow, the Boss stopped going to the Bolshoi—*Boris* was mounted less and less, until it vanished from the repertoire during the war.

And Jurek was my Pretender, my devil of a false tsarevitch. I was drawn to his masquerades and despised them. Perhaps I was my own Pretender, who wanted to be coveted as Stalin's daughter while I sought to erase his memory. But if I clung to Jurek and Jurek's disguises, his devils would wear me down. He could not rest. He picked at whatever sores and wounds I had—his love was shot through with hate. He clawed at my weaknesses while he held my hand.

In my dreams, he appeared with a mustache—and his nose turned into my father's nose, with the nostrils of a wolf. Jurek had come out of the Polish forest, and he would have lured me back inside. I didn't want to live in the dark.

DOWN ON THE FARM, 1967

− 18 −

⌒

O H, THEY INDULGED HER, ALL RIGHT. It's where she always ended up after one of her blackouts. They would sweat the alcohol out of her system with "a cocktail of pharmaceuticals," as her doctors were fond of saying. It was a detox center for the super-rich called Sea Breeze Farm, though there wasn't much of a breeze on its hundred acres outside New Haven.

The Farm wasn't even in the telephone book—it was both a country club and a prison. You couldn't leave the grounds unless you were released, and you couldn't hope to get in unless you had a certain pedigree. "Dear Martha," as she was known at Sea Breeze, was a bit of a maverick. She had been cast out of the *Social Register* after her recent marriage to a Polish parvenu. They never called her Mrs. Kosinski. She was always Mrs. Cuthbert Will, widow of the late CEO and founder of Will Industries, the foremost producer of soft paraffin in the world. She had inherited half his fortune.

"Mr. Cuthbert" was well remembered here. The Petroleum Jelly King was forty years her senior, but whenever she was despondent and couldn't come out of her alcoholic haze, he'd fly her in from headquarters on his personal plane, carry her into Sea Breeze in his own arms. She'd been his devoted secretary, and would have remained loyal, but Cuthbert had to beg her to marry him (after she divorced her spouse and he divorced his). She wanted to keep working for him, but he couldn't have his wife sit behind a desk, like a paid sentry in a polished chair.

It was Cuthbert's mistake; Martha retreated within the walls of the French chateau he had rebuilt near Galveston. She traveled with him from time to time, redecorated his mansion on Robber Island, his hacienda in Santa Fe, but she lost her balance with so little to do. She began suffering blackouts. He bought her a pied-à-terre in Manhattan, a fourteen-room duplex at 740 Park.

She studied modern literature, became a patron of the arts. She studied antique furniture, but she had no passion to trade antiques. She was faithful to her husband, though she saw him less and less. She would sit in her fourteen rooms on Park Avenue, with butlers and maids who had nothing to do but dote on her. She would eat an apple, drink a quart of gin, and spend a month or two at Sea Breeze. She might have committed suicide if the Petroleum Jelly King hadn't succumbed to a heart attack in his eightieth year. His death seemed to rouse her from her stupor. She traveled on her own, stayed in the hotels where she had gone with her husband. Men pursued her. She was the ninth-richest woman in North America.

She had not been to the Farm in a year. She was a devoted widow who performed good deeds and kept away from the sauce. She didn't seem susceptible to fortune hunters and shady men. In fact, there hadn't been the slightest rumor of a love affair. She traveled by herself or with other women of her social set. She was attractive, in her forties, and had the figure of a movie star. The entire staff at See Breeze hoped she would find another "billionaire" like Mr. Cuthbert.

And then this Polack appeared on the scene with his cardboard satchel and his Salvation Army suits. How did he ever get past the doormen at 740 and sneak into her boudoir? He was worse than a gigolo, said Stanislaus, her butler. He was a Jew, though Stanislaus was convinced that he had escaped the slaughterhouses of Europe by pretending to be a pious little Catholic. "I bet you won't find a hair shirt under his jacket, but a Hebrew prayer shawl," Stanislaus had told a therapist at the Farm. And there they were, running around Manhattan and traipsing off to Europe on her wealth, while he was busy paying the tips with wrinkled dollar bills from inside the dark well of his cardboard purse. He went nowhere without that satchel, whether it was the Rainbow Room or the "21" Club. He wouldn't leave it with a hatcheck girl. It sat between his legs during the entire meal.

By now he was Manhattan's new Beau Brummel. Martha had tossed his beggar's wardrobe into the incinerator at 740. She delivered him into the hands of the best Italian tailors. He wore red tuxedos to dinner parties, ruffled shirts, and shoes of exquisite calfskin. But no matter how many Moroccan leather briefcases Martha bought him, he wouldn't get rid of his satchel. And whenever she asked him about it, he would roll his dark eyes and declare, "It's a gift from Gavrila. I cannot betray him, Mimi."

That was his pet name for Martha. *Mimi.* But it didn't explain who Gavrila was. Stanislaus solved the mystery. He discovered that Martha's gigolo had a pseudonym, Joseph Novak, and this Novak was the author of two books about his travels in the Soviet Union. Gavrila appeared in the second book as a political officer and Communist Party boss in Moscow. But Stanislaus didn't believe in Novak's travels or in Gavrila—this Gavrila felt like a false prophet, a voice that an author would invent to give some flavor to his lies.

But Stanislaus was confused: The cardboard satchel seemed authentic enough, and whenever the Polack talked about Gavrila, his eyes lit up with a fever that would have been hard to fake. The butler would listen to him during dinner parties that Martha gave at 740, listen while he decanted the wine. Martha's other guests were in wonder of him and his war stories; they shivered at the horrors he described.

"The Kalmuks raced through the village, killing and looting and tearing the necks off little children. They wore German uniforms, but with their own strange insignias that looked like a wizard's wand. And they didn't have helmets, not a one of them. They had bowler hats with shrunken rooster heads hanging down from the brims. They fit their fat fingers into a child's mittens. Everything about them was maddening to a little boy. But I wasn't so little. I was ten or eleven when the Kalmuks appeared on their ponies. They had all the skills of a saltimbanque—they could ride and shoot, rape a woman and eat a winter pear in one motion. I was appalled and couldn't take my eyes off them. They wanted us to admire them, even while they butchered us, and they would have butchered us all.

"It was almost by accident that the Red Army ran into them— a communications regiment with telegraph equipment as well as guns. They moved so rapidly, like ghosts with telephone wires, that they seldom had to fire a gun. And here were the Kalmuks on a rampage, slaughtering whoever was in their path. The ponies stopped in their tracks when they saw the red stars on the trucks, while the Russians were bewildered by bandits in German uniforms and bowler hats. And then these telegraph boys in their brown tunics let out a war cry and started to slaughter the slaughterers. All the fight had gone out of the saltimbanques. They had raided villages, burned down huts, performed for their victims with the cruelty of consummate clowns, but none of them or their ponies had ever faced a line of guns."

"For God's sake, Jerry," said one of the guests, "where does Gavrila fit in?"

"Oh, he saved my life. A Kalmuk had been about to brain me with the handle of a sword, when Gavrila shot out of nowhere and swatted him off his pony—just like that. I lived with his regiment for months. I was even given a uniform to wear, sewn especially for me by the regimental tailor. But I was more than Gavrila's mascot. He let me borrow books from the little library he had in his rucksack. He said that Comrade Stalin was the greatest reader in the motherland, and that he, Gavrila, would abandon me to the Kalmuks if I didn't become a reader overnight. He taught me all the little knots of Russian grammar in his spare time, and I never wanted to speak a word of Polish again."

"But Jerry," said another of Martha's guests, all flushed with the wine that Stanislaus had decanted at the table. "I thought you were mute during the war?"

"I was, but my voice came back gradually with Gavrila. He would have taken me with him to Moscow if my parents hadn't found me—it was the biggest disappointment of my life."

Martha nearly leapt out of her chair, Stanislaus recalled to the staff at Sea Breeze.

"That is heartless and cruel," she said. "And I won't listen to another syllable of your story."

The Polish charmer smiled and kissed her hand. "But it's the truth, Mimi, so help me God. From that moment I dreamt of one thing—moving to Moscow and having Gavrila as my teacher for life. But the Gavrila I visited when I was still in high school wasn't the same guy who could destroy Kalmuks with a swat of his hand. He'd grown fat in peacetime. I loved him, but Gavrila seemed lost without his regiment, without his boys. He smelled of garlic. He wore a blue suit that must have been sitting on a warehouse shelf with a thousand other suits for minor Soviet chiefs. It seemed to rot on him . . . and it's because of Gavrila's garlic and blue suit, ladies and gentlemen, that I'm with you here tonight."

Stanislaus was still suspicious. He wondered if there had ever been a Gavrila. But it didn't really matter as long as his own mistress was amused. She traveled with her gigolo, went on long trips, and one morning she arrived at 740 married to him—it was in January of '62. And even Stanislaus had to admit that Martha had a sudden radiance; she shimmered like the softest of lanterns. Her servants "forgave" Martha for being in love with "*Jerry*," as she called him. They had not seen her this happy in a long time. There were no more alcoholic binges where she wouldn't bother to dress, no more visits to Sea Breeze in the middle of the night. But it didn't last.

By the end of '63, most of the radiance was gone. She had the frazzled look of a drunken millionairess who was fast approaching fifty. The binges had returned, and the blackouts. Martha's new husband had to drive her to Sea Breeze in the Lincoln Continental she had bought him, with the cardboard satchel still at his side. He wasn't harsh with his wife. He would hold her hand and read her Russian fairy tales. The night staff was amazed at his tenderness. He could calm her whenever she had a fit, scold her when she had to be scolded.

But he was always bribing people with his dollar bills, and he seduced one of the night nurses. There might have been a scandal, but Sea Breeze couldn't afford to lose Martha as a client—it was her benefice that had paid for a new wing. And so they tolerated his lecheries and his dollar bills. She had divorced him a year ago, in '66, and the staff hoped they were rid of the Polack for good. But the blackouts were more and more frequent; she lived between Manhattan and New Haven in a kind of hypnotic trance. And when she was utterly out of control, they had to call Kosinski.

He was driving a Bentley now, and he would often appear with one or two women in the car—they looked like prostitutes, or transvestites, several of the nurses noticed. He would always leave them in the Bentley while he rambled into Sea Breeze, wearing a velvet suit. He no longer had a pen name. He'd become a celebrated novelist, had written *The Painted Bird,* a tantalizing book in the opinion of those staffers who had read past the first ten pages.

But there he was, clutching his cardboard satchel, like someone with half his history secreted inside. He was the miracle man of the moment. He was the one who could quiet her. Sometimes he would comb her hair, and even with the medication that had disfigured her—swelled her mouth and turned her tongue a little green—her eyes would glisten and a little of her radiance would come back.

"Mimi, you mustn't break any mirrors. It will bring you the rottenest luck. And if you threaten to bankrupt this institution, where will you go when you misbehave?"

"Inside your pocket," she said.

"And what will you do in there?"

"Play with your prick."

"And if the doctors hear you say that?" he said.

"They'll think I'm perfectly sober. A wife who cherishes conjugal relations with her husband."

"But Mimi, we're not married anymore."

"That's a minor detail," she said. "Call the chaplain, Jerry, and I'll marry you again."

"Then why did you divorce me in the first place?"

"Because I had a husband who liked to wander far afield. I didn't mind your having a mistress on the side, and fucking two or three whores at a time, arranging your little sex parties, but you never included me. Darling, don't I have a cunt?"

"Where did you ever get such a filthy mouth?"

"From you," she told him.

"But it's bed talk. It shouldn't go beyond the satin sheets."

"I prefer bed talk outside of bed—Jurek, will you fuck me or not?"

"In front of the nurses, darling?"

"Who cares? I support this nunnery."

"Nunnery? It's a rehabilitation center."

"A nunnery," she insisted. "It doesn't give a shit about my sex. All I am is a machine who writes the checks. And if you don't fuck me this minute, darling, I'll leave you out of my will."

He laughed, but it wasn't the laugh of a hyena. It was a quiet sound.

"It's naughty of you to threaten me, dear. I'll never be rich, but I am a writer who earns royalties."

"I could spit your royalties into a sink and they would disappear down the pipes."

She licked her lips with her green tongue and began to sob without control. He stroked her head and she quieted down.

"I'm a witch, I really arm."

He rocked her in his arms. She fell asleep, babbling to herself. He distributed dollar bills and returned to the Bentley with his cardboard satchel.

– 19 –

~~

THEY COULD HEAR HER BABBLE DAY AND NIGHT. It was an incessant song, punctuated with a laugh that was close to the cackle of a mother hen. She babbled even while the night nurse bathed her, or while she smoked one of her filter tips, or had her filet of sole prepared by Sea Breeze's gourmet chef, or was lifted onto her pony, Proud Margaret, tame as a carriage horse. They would strap her in and lead Proud Margaret by the nose; on a good morning, she and her pony might cover half an acre of ground. But she wouldn't stop babbling.

It had something to do with books.

"Be a dear and lend me a cig," she said. She could have been addressing her pony. And then she turned about to cluck at the sky, and God knows who her interlocutor was now. But you only had to listen. She was looking for some fabric in her own past, was weaving a tapestry while she rode Proud Margaret at a snail's pace. The tapestry was about a certain year—1960—when she was touring Europe and didn't even bother to dance. *There was no shortage of suitors, my dears.* Counts by the hundred, Swiss industrialists who mentioned marriage before Martha had a chance to sit down. *I read Nabokov on the train to Nice.* She preferred his tangled garden to the talk of a suitor. She couldn't stop thinking of her library, shelf after shelf of books that had never been cataloged, never been touched. She was Minnie, the Tartar Queen, who would swallow the entire stock of bookstores that were about to close. Minnie's husband had taught her well. "You must look them in the eye, and the price will go down and down."

She did much more than that. The Tartar Queen tantalized these bookish men, drew them out of their cubbyholes, and scratched the sums that she owed them in her crabbed hand. But she never bothered with the books. Martha built a library and hadn't even gone inside. She had Stanislaus stack the books on the shelves. He would look at her with the insufferable air of a servant who was conscious of every penny she had.

"Should I alphabetize them, Mum?"

And she would have to say, "Stannie, shut up! You're becoming a real pain in the ass."

But she shouldn't have been so blasé with her own butler. She soon had a monstrosity in her flat, a tower of Babel that she had helped create. And when she had a teensy-weensy too much to drink, Martha could hear the books whisper among themselves. That's why she went off to Europe. It was to escape the blitz. But she confided in her butler first.

"Stannie, can't you hear that whispering? How do you keep sane?"

"I have earplugs, Mum. I sleep as sound as a saint."

While she was gone, she had her girlfriends scout for some miserable graduate student who could bring order to her books. They found a perfect candidate, a Polish émigré who was studying the social sciences at Columbia. And he was still in the library when she returned to the States. It was autumn or winter, and the whole of Park Avenue was in the middle of a heating oil strike—deliverers stopped delivering, or perhaps 740 had run out of oil. Her young cataloger was standing on the library ladder, wrapped in

an abominable squirrel-hair coat. It looked like a live animal with
bald spots. Martha was so alarmed by this coat that she didn't even
bother to introduce herself. She was callous with him.

"Kosinski, you mustn't come here in such a coat. It could frighten
pregnant women in the building and make them miscarry."

She was startled by her own preposterous remarks. She didn't
know of one pregnant woman at 740 Park. Fending off all those
European suitors must have sharpened her imagination. But this
cataloger had the balls to turn his back and slide along the ladder
that led to her Babel of books. Finally he consented to glance at
her, with pure poison in his dark eyes. It embarrassed Martha, and
she broke out in hives.

"Are you Mrs. Will's secretary?" he asked. "I myself have not
met madam. I wear this coat in homage to Stalin. Stalin wore a
coat like mine summer and winter. He found it when he was exiled
in Siberia. He never took it off. He washed with his coat on, made
love while wearing it, went hunting in his coat."

"Enough!" she said. "Why are you so enamored of a mass
murderer?"

The hives began to itch, but Martha wouldn't rub her arms and
legs in front of this hyena in squirrel hair. He began to chastise her.

"You and I have had a different upbringing, young lady. Stalin's
soldiers saved my life."

The hives vanished and Martha began to blush. No one had
called her *young lady* in a long, long time. Martha was old enough
to be his aunt. *Young lady.* She liked it! And he hadn't meant to flat-
ter her. But she played out the part of her own secretary.

"Mum would like to know how you are cataloging her books? Is
it by subject or alphabetical order?"

"By interest," he said.

When she asked her arrogant dark-eyed cataloger to explain

himself, he climbed down from the ladder. He seemed much taller now that he wasn't hunched over on his wooden perch. But he wore the same French cologne as some of her suitors. She did not care for its tart aroma—it reminded her of oversweet flowers. She had to endure him and that stink.

"I cannot catalog books without having a peek inside the covers. It took me a month to wade through madam's library."

"You read every book?" Martha asked, trying to mask her astonishment.

"Not every line. A chapter will do . . . unless I fall into the dream of a book, and then I might glance at a second chapter and a third."

"And the rest of madam's library?"

"Stockpiled," he said. "I found an ideal place for them. A walk-in closet in madam's bedroom. I piled them near her shoes. She can incinerate them or sell these worthless books."

She had to close her eyes and count, or she might have slapped his face and had him barred from 740. When she opened her eyes again, she was twice as angry.

"You're a cataloger, not a couturier. Stanislaus permitted you into Mum's bedroom?"

"I don't need his permission. A butler knows nothing of books."

"And did you catalog her blouses and sweaters while you were in the mood?"

He sniffed about with his beak of a nose, suspicious of a secretary who was such a shrew.

"I am not a burglar—what's your name?"

"Charlotte Haze," she said, spitting out the name of Lolita's mom in the Nabokov novel she liked best.

There was a slight ripple in his forehead, no other sign. She decided to rip into his arrogance, fillet him and his squirrel-hair coat. But she'd caught a chill in this icy flat, and she started to sneeze. He removed his coat and furled it around her shoulders like a cape. She wanted to scream. The coat was drenched in that awful perfume.

"Cataloger," she demanded, hoping to trap him into some extravagant claim, "which of Mum's books do you like best?"

He laughed at her, exhibiting his large teeth.

"My dear Charlotte Haze," he said, "Madam has a fixation on one book—I counted eleven copies of *Lolita,* with and without dust jackets. I consigned the copies without dust jackets to madam's closet. I do admire that book. My favorite character isn't Humbert Humbert or Clare Quilty . . . it's Charlotte Haze. She gets short shrift in the novel. Trapped in a love triangle with her own daughter. But I smell another triangle, another trap, involving you, me, and *Mum.* Do you like to fool around with names and identities? Or was *Mum* so infatuated with the book, she had to hire another Charlotte Haze?"

Martha was shivering now. "You really are an unbearable man. Do you often make fun of your own employers?"

He clicked his heels like one of the counts she had met. "I will leave this minute."

"You can't," she said. "Kosinski, I'm wearing your coat."

Both of them laughed, and they whirled around each other as if they were dancing. And Martha realized that this was the first time since she'd gone to London with Cuthbert on their last trip that she wanted to dance.

— 20 —

$$\backsim$$

STILL SHE BABBLED, EVEN AFTER THE ONE SIP of sherry they allowed her. She babbled in the hydrotherapy room, where she sat in the whirlpool machine with a rubber cap on her head—it reminded her of the cap she had worn at swim meets in high school. And after they dried her and let her sit on the fenced-in veranda outside her room, Martha seemed to be involved in some drama with several voices.

"Our dear Martha's a bit of a ham," they laughed among themselves. "She has all the speaking parts." But they didn't try to shake her out of that long verbal dream. It was only when her butler came to Sea Breeze that Martha stopped babbling to herself.

"Stannie," she cooed. "I suppose you've come to have me sign a million checks."

"We have to pay your staff, Mum. Even the most loyal maid must eat once in a while."

He liked using the royal *we* with her. Stanislaus probably had better schooling than she ever did. Cuthbert had stolen him from some dying duke. Stanislaus was raised among the nobility and didn't much like Americans. But he was devoted to her. And he had a rage against Jerry, thought she never should have married him.

"My God," she said, "you're much better about books than I am. How would you rate him as a writer?"

"Rate whom, Mum?"

"Don't play *his* game, Stannie. . . . My Polish ex with the pointy ears."

"He's a sorcerer, Mum. That's how I would rate him. All his gifts, all his talents, are tied up with mischief. And since he writes with several hands, I can no longer tell what is really his."

"Don't talk riddles, Stannie. What do you mean?"

"Gabriela," he said, and when he saw that frozen lip of hers and the bitterness that consumed her face, he was sorry he had said it. Little Gabriela had been Kosinski's amanuensis and sexual slave, though it wasn't quite clear whether she was his slave at all. He must have picked her up among his Polish connections. She wasn't there during the first days of courtship. Perhaps he was only hiding her. But after Mum had married her sorcerer, Gabriela suddenly appeared. She was a stunner, with raven red hair, and when she walked up Mum's marble steps, the maids pitied Mum and despised themselves.

Gabriela was barely five feet tall, buxom, with tresses that reached her rear end, like some medieval maiden. She never flirted with the sorcerer. She would closet herself with him in his study. And when she ventured outside to ask for a carrot or a piece of cake, she was always clutching a manuscript and a green pencil. She would crouch under her own crossed legs on Mum's white sofa and mutter sentences to herself. Then she would mark up a page with the pencil in her hand.

Stanislaus never spied on her, though he might have for Mum's sake. But Gabriela seemed to want company. And he didn't have to prod.

"Would you believe it? I'm not allowed to take a chapter out of here. He searches under my bra. I never met such a secretive man.

He thinks his sentences are sacred, but he couldn't write one page in English all on his own."

"Miss Gabriela, you could always quit."

"That's the problem. I can't. I'm hooked on the son of a bitch. He's my Dracula."

And Stanislaus believed her. A bloodsucking sorcerer with pointy ears.

Gabriela would undergo sudden changes. She'd show up dressed as a man, her long hair pulled back and hidden under a hat. She'd talk in a husky voice, which frightened the maids. She could have been possessed by demons, and Stanislaus lacked the courage and the determination to drive them out of her. Then the husky voice would disappear, and she was Gabriela again, the pint-size bombshell. But the stability didn't last. She would show up with her hair shorn, like Joan of Arc. She would have terrible fights in the sorcerer's study, descend the stairs without a stitch, blue welts on her arms, in a state of hysteria. But Stanislaus was reluctant to get near a naked girl. It was Mum who would quiet her down. Then the three of them would go off to the "21" Club, the sorcerer with his cardboard satchel, Gabriela in a borrowed gown.

Stanislaus or one of the maids would find them next morning, with Mum sleeping in her mask at the foot of the bed. It was the oddest ménage à trois he had ever seen. The sorcerer was somewhere at the far side of the bed, while Gabriela would be lying in a silk nightgown, holding Mum's hand. They looked like three errant children unable to have the simplest liaison.

They squabbled all the time. Gabriela slit her wrists—nothing *too* serious. Mum's own doctor appeared at 740 in the middle of the night. Mum conspired with Stanislaus to move Gabriela into a residence for single women, a "nunnery," where the sorcerer couldn't find her. He screamed at Stanislaus, who tossed him down

Mum's marble stairs. Mum went on one of her binges while the sorcerer was away somewhere. Stanislaus phoned Sea Breeze, and a limo came to collect her. When the sorcerer returned from his trip, Stanislaus had him all to himself.

He gave no parties, nor could he get near Gabriela. He would lock himself in his study—an odd, barren corner with two desks and two cots—and come down to dinner promptly at seven in a plum-colored coat. It was Stanislaus who filled the sorcerer's wine-glass with buttermilk. The sorcerer glared at him during the meal.

"You don't approve of me. You think I'm not good enough for her."

"I think nothing of the kind. I'm a butler, sir, and butlers are not paid to think."

"You'd strangle me in my bed if Mum gave the signal."

Stanislaus wasn't sure what devil had gotten into him. "I suppose I would," he blurted, and the sorcerer smiled.

"Stanislaus, have some wine. I insist."

"I am not permitted to imbibe in the presence of my employer or her guests."

"But I'm not a guest. I'm married to Mimi, or haven't you noticed?

"I have noticed, sir."

"Can't you call me Jerry or Jurek, or whatever name leaps into your mind?"

"Sorcerer," Stanislaus said. "If I might take the liberty, sir."

"Is that what the maids call me?"

"And the doormen, sir. That is your name in the building. I was the one who supplied it. The responsibility is all mine. You might want to voice a complaint with Mum."

"But I have no wish to complain."

"Then I will have that drink," Stanislaus said.

And it was like slumming with the enemy. Stanislaus finished half a bottle of Pomerol that Mum had kept in her own little "cave" under the stairs, while the sorcerer gulped his buttermilk. The buttermilk made him tipsy. They were no longer sitting in Mum's prize comb-back chairs. They'd climbed onto her enormous oak table and sat there, six feet apart.

"Sorcerer, I would like to strangle you in your bed without a signal from Mum. And one of these days I will. . . . Would you mind very much if I asked you a question?"

"Strangle me first," said the sorcerer. "I always ask a woman to strangle me while we're making love. That, my friend, is the secret behind the best orgasms."

"But I am not a woman, sir, and I doubt that even your sorcery could turn me into one."

"But you could pretend."

"One of these days I will. . . . Sorcerer, does this Gavrila of yours really exist? The Christ-like Soviet savior who suddenly arrives in Poland and rescues a mute little boy from barbarians. I find that hard to believe. Not even Dostoyevsky would have dared pull such a trick. Did you know that his novels would often come to him in long hallucinations? He dictated all his dreams to his second wife."

"Ah, you've picked through Mum's shelves like a man robbing a grave and settled on Madame Dostoyevskaya's memoirs. And you believe her nonsense. Madame was a whore. She sucked off men at the train station to pay the bills. She pimped for her precious Fyodor, found him young girls to play with."

"Lies," said Stanislaus, who longed to cover his ears and kill the sorcerer. "There is no mention of such things in her book. She was a loving wife who sacrificed herself to her husband's art."

"He was a pedophile who raped ten-year-olds and hid behind his wife's skirts."

"You are no sorcerer, sir. You are a swine. And I will not listen."

But Stanislaus sat on the table and poured another glass of Pomerol. He was stuck in the sorcerer's invisible strings. Now he understood how her Polish protégé had driven Mum to distraction. The sorcerer continued to smile and smile.

"Lenin once said that all butlers who read books should be shot, because they are maggots who feast on other people's minds. But I am not as ruthless as Lenin. I will not punish you, Stanislaus, for having feasted on my own flesh. . . . I wouldn't be alive without Gavrila. Whatever compassion I have left comes from him. He ravished no one. Peasants offered their own wives to Gavrila. He shared their potatoes, nothing else. He had the regiment's doctor attend to boys and old men with running sores. He parted with whatever medicine he had. And in my own mind, Stanislaus, I am still with Gavrila's regiment."

⌐

MUM'S CHECKBOOK WAS AS LONG AS A LEDGER. It wouldn't fit into a briefcase. Stanislaus had carried it all the way from 740 in a huge shopping bag. He read out the names and exact figures to her while she sat on the veranda. She devoted a full hour to signing checks in a musical motion, as if she were savoring her own signature. Stanislaus had to write in the date—March 11, 1967. And it was Stanislaus who tore the signed checks from that ledger and deposited them in a cardboard envelope with accordion folders.

"Stannie, should I write a check for *her*?"

"Mum, I don't—"

"Her, her—Gabriela. Do you think the Polish one loved Gabriela more than he loved me? I doubt that he loved me at all. He's like a swooping bird that picks up carrion."

"I wouldn't call yourself carrion, Mum."

"Then what would you call me? A smart aleck? I get dirty looks from my neighbors when I'm sober enough to see them. They must think I kept a bordello on the sixth floor. I'm surprised the building's lawyer hasn't served me with a summons."

"They couldn't kick you out, Mum. I wouldn't let them."

"An army of two. Mimi the alcoholic and her butler . . . Of course they can't kick me out. But if they pester me long enough, I'll have to sell my shares in the building back to them. I'll become a bag lady. I'll walk the streets with my butler and my seven maids."

She was silent and soon fell into a sound sleep. Stanislaus covered her with a blanket. Her "episodes," her periods of oblivion, had gotten worse and worse. The sorcerer had once called them "Mimi's little suicides." But Stanislaus didn't have the sorcerer's poetic temperament. Mum was in the middle of a voyage, her own sea of despair. The sorcerer had charmed her for a little while, loved Mum as much as a snake could love. He wasn't a gigolo, or he would have held on to her for dear life. He was a seducer who had to crush the very carapace he had bothered to build. Mum could have been his "ticket," but he was much too perverse. She couldn't control him with her wealth. He might have luxuriated in the suits and cars she could buy him, but they were his props, pieces to costume himself with. Had he really been a sybarite, he wouldn't have turned his little retreat at 740 into a monk's cell.

His currency was pain—pain he inflicted upon others and himself. He was like a wounded animal that thrived on the smell of blood. Mum's socialite friends despised the sorcerer, said he was a little kike. Yet even as they mocked him, he was defiant. He carried that cardboard satchel around as a badge. He could have been throwing the dollar bills into their eyes.

Speak of the devil! There he was on the main path of Sea Breeze sanitarium. The celebrated author in plum-colored satin pants and a new coiffure—a crown of black curls covered the sinister points of his ears. But Stanislaus knew how much of Gabriela's green pencil had gone into *The Painted Bird*. She couldn't have invented the horrors inside his head, but Gabriela had helped shape the sorcerer's endless scream.

"Hullo, Stanislaus. Did you forget your promise to strangle me in my bed? . . . I have been waiting three years. How's Mimi?"

"Asleep, Sorcerer."

"Her doctor told me that she's had a very bad spell—talks to herself continuously, mentions my name. But God knows if she still can bear to look at my face."

"It's not your face, Sorcerer, that troubles her. Your face is fine."

"Then it's the stone in my heart."

"Or the hot coals you use to warm other women. But mine is only a butler's point of view."

Stanislaus waved good-bye and continued along the path.

"I have no hot coals," the sorcerer had to shout into his back.

"Sorry, sir, I misspoke," Stanislaus mumbled, and kept walking.

–21–

N Florence, he discovered a tailor shop that would outfit
him with a motley of costumes, while she walked the streets of
a whole city in burnt sienna, with flat-roofed buildings that were
like a museum built right into the countryside—it must have
been 1963. Florence was unsettling to her after the mayhem of
Manhattan. It was a town of beautiful boxes. She marched into a
gelateria and had a little pot of pistachio ice cream that was like
no ice cream she had ever tasted—she would move to Florence
and drown in a tub of green gelato.

But her monster of a husband had put her on a diet.

"Mimi darling, you're getting a little too fat. I'll have to find
you a sedan chair to climb the hills."

"There are no hills in Florence," she protested. That hardly
mattered to him. She was condemned to gobbling lettuce leaves
at the best trattoria in town. She couldn't lash out at him, because
he sat like a little saint who gobbled his own lettuce leaves. Martha had almost never seen him eat an actual meal. At dinner parties, he would swear that as a wild boy he had learned to live on
roots. But Stanislaus had once seen him stuffing cheese biscuits
into his face before he sat down to dinner. That tale endeared
him to her—Jurek's secret gluttony. And now she could indulge
in some gluttony of her own at the gelateria.

She wished she had never told him about that Florentine tailor shop. Martha's friends had sworn her to secrecy—it was where they had the most fashionable uniforms cut for members of their households. But she had spilled the name of the shop to Jurek in a moment of weakness over a glass of wine. And her new husband had a field day.

Jurek walked out of the shop wearing a general's uniform. Martha was stunned when soldiers and policemen came to a halt, saluted him, and called her "La Grande Signora." But that was only the beginning of his masquerade. He strolled with her into the bar at the Baglioni in a costume that had all the ridiculous earmarks of an Eastern European fire marshal—a plumed hat, a silver dagger, a short cape—and every single eyebrow wrinkled up a bit. The fire marshal ordered aquavit.

"Darling," he said, "once I have a sip, you'll have to bring me back to the hotel. My temperature will drop—it could be fatal."

"Then I forbid you to drink it!"

He gulped the aquavit and his face turned blue. Martha wanted to call an ambulance, but her husband insisted that she escort him to the Bristol like some baby-sitter.

"Darling, you must get me to talk, or I might land in a coma."

That frozen blueness in his face was beyond melodrama. His back scrunched over, and he could have been four feet tall.

"Tell me about Hemingway," she said. "Wasn't he stationed here in Florence during the First World War?"

"No!" he said with a violent shiver. "It's not like the Second War, when he *liberated* Paris in a jeep and took over the Ritz. He shot his own room with a machine gun."

"But we stayed in Hemingway's room, didn't we, darling? I remember. You tied my hands to the bedpost and we made love for three hours."

"Listen! He was a buffoon at the Ritz. But it wasn't always that way. In 1918, he was an ambulance driver—not even that. He delivered chocolate to soldiers at the front. He had a charmed existence, with shells landing everywhere except on him. Then he was blown up, and he could feel all the life leave his body. But the dead man returned. He woke up at a hospital, but it wasn't in Florence, darling; it was in Milan, and he had fifty pieces of shrapnel in his buttocks. He fell in love with a beautiful American nurse, Agnes von Kurowsky."

"Darling, she doesn't sound American to me. Did he fuck her on the hospital floor?"

"Mimi, pay attention! He didn't fuck her at all. His ass was broken, for God's sake. And she was in love with another man, an unctuous Italian officer."

"Then I'm no longer interested."

His face turned even bluer, and his feet began to flutter. "I'm sorry," she said, panicking as she propped him up with her arms. "Tell me—tell me, darling, why you are so mysterious about your uniforms, and why you are compelled to wear them? It's not as if we're utterly unknown. I've been staying as the Bristol for years—I could command any suite with one telephone call. And I feel a bit ridiculous running around Florence as the wife of a Serbian fire marshal."

He broke free of her. "I'm not a Serbian fire marshal. I'm a Polish air attaché. And you couldn't possibly know the significance of a uniform. It's not an indictment, darling. It's the truth. You didn't grow up in a whirlwind, where the landscape shifted every five minutes. You grew up with pieces of cake and postmen handing you letters that didn't even have a stamp. But there were no bakers in the Polish woods, and the postmen I met as a boy were partisans and thieves who stole from everybody. But a man in a uniform—any uniform—was looked upon with wonder. If he had a chevron on his coat, he could have been a messenger from some important prince. The Nazis didn't even have to kill a man. They wore their black uniforms with a death's-head insignia, and entire villages surrendered without a fight. A uniform broke their will. A uniform meant sanity in an insane world."

"But we're in Florence, darling, and Florence isn't insane."

"It is," he said, "if you look under its veil."

She was no longer listening; she had lured him into the lobby of the Bristol. Martha sat him in a green velvet chair while she secured their key from the concierge. The key was as large as her hand and had a purple glow under the Bristol's chandelier. Hotel guests saluted Jurek even as he sat dazed, with shivering blue lips. She managed to get him up to their suite, and while she undressed him, hot coffee and Italian biscuits arrived.

Martha had administered to him once before. She couldn't understand his curious reaction to alcohol, but hot coffee and a biscuit would revive him from what he called his "sugar comas." She fed him coffee from a teal blue cup and broke off a bit of biscuit for him to chew. He whispered something to her in Polish. It wasn't a lover's cajoling voice—it was the voice of a child.

Then he looked into her eyes and said, "*Matka*, hold my hand."

Was he thinking of his mother? He didn't like to speak of his parents. But he'd had one little outburst, a week or so into their marriage, when he discovered that his father had died. He cursed and screamed, wept bitterly, and then stared at the wall. Martha didn't know what to do about this catatonic condition. She telephoned his Polish friends, other exiles who hadn't landed on their feet quite as well as Jurek. They were a gloomy lot and called her "the little *kapitalistka*" behind her back (so said Stanislaus). They were envious of her marble staircase, envious of her maids, envious of Jurek's new clothes; they would smirk and raid the vodka in the fridge, but they knew how to tease their Jurek, to make him laugh. They pilfered ashtrays, spoons, and cigarette lighters from the apartment, but Martha considered this a worthwhile hazard.

They were poets, translators, and freedom fighters who lived on the largesse of others—foundations or rich friends; and when they couldn't wheedle or beg, they stole. Stanislaus considered them gangsters and would have barred then from 740, but she was attracted to their recklessness; they were raw in a way Martha could never be.

When they arrived in their own squirrel-hair coats, sniffing about, raping the walls with their greedy eyes, Jurek wouldn't greet them.

"Darling, they're your friends. I thought . . ."

"Mimi, send then away."

Stanislaus fed them in the kitchen, gave each one a doggie bag, and shoved them out the door. Martha assumed her husband would wander upstairs and lie down in his study. But he insisted on going to "21." And his gloom was completely gone. He was done with mourning, or perhaps he had pulled it so deep inside himself that there wasn't even a trace. He danced with her. He chatted with her girlfriends, who had come over to their table at "21." She was dying to talk to him about *Matka,* but she never did. He wouldn't attend his father's funeral in Lodz, though Martha offered to accompany him to Poland.

"I cannot go back there," he said. "I'm a wanted man."

She didn't want to hear another of his tales about the Polish secret service, with Jurek as a rogue agent who had to watch his step wherever he went.

"I understand, darling," she said, like a woman mouthing words in a dream. "A wanted man."

And then, out of the blue, *Matka* herself appeared.

Now that she was a widow, Elzbieta Kosinska decided to visit her son in New York. Martha thought that Jurek would discourage her. But he was oddly passive about the visit, as if fate had him by the balls and there was little he could do about it.

They met her at the airport. Martha didn't know what to expect. Jurek had been so stingy on the subject of Elzbieta. "My mother was beautiful and she had big breasts." Where was *Matka* while Jurek roamed the countryside and ate roots during the war? She was a concert pianist who liked to polish her nails, Jurek had said.

Martha saw a woman in her sixties with a slight stoop. She was wearing a coat from Saks that Martha and Jurek had sent her. She didn't look like the victim of any cold war. Her makeup was as "invisible" as Martha's own. Her face was much softer than her son's. She didn't have his prominent beak. Her mouth, even with its pale gloss, had a measure of fullness that Jurek's didn't have. But she had the same dark eyes of a scavenger, someone on the prowl.

Martha looked for signs of affection between mother and son, and found none. This meeting, after six years of separation, seemed rehearsed. There was a perfunctory kiss, but Madame Kosinska didn't rub his shoulder or lean on him. Martha felt no hunger between them. It could have been the chance encounter of an estranged husband and wife. Jurek once boasted that he had made love to his mother when he was a teenager in Lodz. Martha didn't believe him. It sounded like the rough imaginings of a pornographic novel. He had meant to excite her during their own lovemaking.

"Darling," he'd said, "I couldn't stop kissing her cunt."

"Jerry, I don't want to hear about it."

"Then why are you tingling?"

Stanislaus had been right. She *was* married to a sorcerer. "Did she seduce you, darling?"

"Yes—no—yes. It was sudden. My father had already had several heart attacks. He shrank into his own skin. He must have floated off to the chess club in Lodz. And I wasn't a shy, pimply swain. I had plenty of girlfriends in high school. But it wasn't so easy to maneuver them into bed. My sweethearts all lived at home with their mothers and sisters and brothers. And the parks were filled with hooligans. So I needed a strategy, and I found it in my camera. I would go off on photography excursions and seduce secretaries right off the street. They were more resourceful than high school girls, even if they still lived at home. I fucked them in cellars, in backyards, in linen closets, and I didn't have to concern myself with the whiff of my own mother."

Martha's throat had turned dry. "Go on, you monster. What happened?"

"But she must have smelled these other women on my clothes—you can't bathe, darling, after an encounter in a coal bin. She was curious at first, then a little more than curious. She came out of the bathroom wearing a towel that didn't even cover her privates. She hadn't oiled herself or anything, hadn't pranced in front of me, but the musk of her breasts was maddening. Mama could see the confused fury in my eyes. I followed her into the bedroom and lived between her legs for half an hour."

And here was the aging diva in Martha's duplex at 740, Madame Kosinska, come from Poland to see how her son had settled on Park Avenue with the sultry widow of the Petroleum Jelly King. Martha felt a sudden embarrassment about her sexual hunger, as if she had to vie for Jurek's favors with his own mother—it was ridiculous and sordid, and she didn't believe a word of Jurek's little tale. He'd told it to enchant her, to crawl into her skin, and turn her into his slave, but he'd only half-succeeded. Her image of Jurek in bed with Elzbieta had evaporated quite quickly.

Martha saw a fierce, wrinkled woman who might have been the lioness of Lodz before the war. But when Martha presented her at little cocktail parties, Elzbieta wouldn't play the piano for any of the guests. "Please, my fingers . . . I forget the keys." And then, in the middle of a meal, she would rise like a somnambulist, sit down at the piano, play half of Chopin's *heroique* Polonaise, and return to her lamb chop. It was a move that Jurek himself might have orchestrated, and Martha began to suspect that Madame Kosinska was some kind of complex doll on a string. She never interrupted Jurek, or contradicted him, when he told his little fables of abandonment in the Polish forest, and all Martha could do was wonder, Where the hell were Madame Kosinska and her husband? Had they run off to Switzerland? Why, why, why had they thrown Jurek to the wolves?

Perhaps the very idea of *The Painted Bird* had begun in Martha's living room at 740, and the tale could only have risen out of him in the presence of his mother. It might have been part of a pact they had formed a long time ago, a pact of lies—no, she struggled for a better word. Not lies, but masks or evasions. And while Elzbieta listened as Jurek told of how he had been tossed into a well of manure, or nearly had his nose bitten off, Martha realized that there was no point at all in getting Elzbieta alone in some corner. Martha couldn't break into that relentless armor of mother and son. And it was at this moment, more than a year into their marriage, that Martha knew she would not be able to endure a lifetime with her sorcerer.

A ND WHAT DID SHE HAVE WITHOUT HIM? A romance with a bottle that ended in blackouts and oblivion. She'd even gone to AA meetings at the little church near Fifth. "Hello, my name is Mimi, the Tartar Queen, and I'm an alcoholic." Who would have recognized her in dark glasses and a mink coat? But all the testimonials and readings of the Lord's Prayer and the furtive clutching of hands couldn't keep her sober. She'd had a short, brutal affair with a banker she met at AA. He was a sadistic prick, and Stanislaus had to throw him out the back door, sit him in a garbage barrel, and have him sent down to the basement on the service car.

She'd become a kleptomaniac in her spare time. She found a man's black shirt at Bloomingdale's that would have been dead perfect on a fascist dictator . . . or Jurek. She stuffed the shirt under her blouse and would have escaped with it to Lexington Avenue if Stanislaus hadn't stood near the entrance with *her* checkbook and a bundle of cash.

Martha was in a rage. "I cannot bear it when you follow me around. I'm not a convict, you know. Are you listening, Stannie?"

"I am. But I'd rather pay for your purchases than have to trot down to Greenwich Avenue, Mum, and visit you at the Women's House of Detention."

"Don't be ridiculous."

But she allowed Stannie to pay for the black shirt.

"He's my sugar daddy," she told the clerk. "And my pimp—he finds me men to sleep with."

And a week later, she was back at the Farm. It mystified her why Stannie hadn't quit. He could have worked for the best families in Manhattan, and he chose to remain with a derelict who had bombed out of AA. The staff fed her applesauce with a teaspoon.

She dozed out on the veranda and dreamt of an albino deer leaping across the lawn. *I'm that deer*, she told herself. *I'm a renegade with pink skin imprisoned inside a lawn without limits*. And when she opened her eyes, Martha could see the sorcerer.

"Darling, where's your uniform? You won't be able to free me from this pestilential place without your Serbian fire marshal's tunic."

"Mimi, I told you a million times. I'm a Polish air attaché, but not this afternoon. I didn't come here to free you, darling."

"Then to punish me for divorcing you and leaving you threadbare, without one black shirt."

"I'm not threadbare, darling. I receive royalties from eleven countries. I have won fellowships and prizes."

"Yes, yes, my little painted bird. Then why did you come here, Jurek?"

"To sit quietly with you and hold your hand."

"And that will make my loins quiver, I suppose. Darling, if you don't need my money or my love, then all I am is a useless hag from another life of yours. Couldn't we start all over again, even with your royalties? You could pretend to be that graduate student in a squirrel-hair coat, and I could have you catalog my books."

"Shhh!" he said. "I command you."

"Yes, I love commands."

"Shhh!" he said, and the sorcerer clutched her hand.

But she wasn't silent for long. "Tell me a story, Jurek."

He looked at her with his Gypsy eyes. "I'm not a spigot, darling. I can't turn the tap on and off, on and off. The stories have to end."

"About Gavrila," she said, imitating the Continental *r* that he had given up. He didn't need it now that he was a celebrated author.

"Jurek, did you really get that cardboard satchel from Gavrila?"

"No," he said. She had gotten him to laugh.

"I picked it up in Poland just before I came to America—it reminded me of him. I would have been lonely without it."

"And you didn't sleep with your mother, did you, darling?"

"Yes," he said, with a silken purr. "I often slept in mama's bed when I was a little boy."

"You know what I mean, darling—sleep with her the way you slept with me once upon a time."

But he wouldn't commit himself.

"Jurek, how do you ever fall asleep at night? You must stumble over your own stories."

"I was trained to be a liar," he said. "Trained by my father."

"Did he have a double life, my darling, as a secret assassin?"

"Papa didn't do much killing away from the chessboard. But he saved my skin. I couldn't have gotten through the war without a million lies. Papa burnt that into me. But we never got along. . . . Martha, it's time to sleep."

"Lie down with me, Jurek. I promise not to seduce you. I don't even remember how to seduce."

And he got into bed with all his clothes on; he felt like an animal with woolen skin. It calmed her. She shut her eyes. But Martha couldn't even pretend to sleep. Her mind wasn't a Moviola, a magic machine that could edit in and edit out the images of her life. It was more like a monster that loved to drift. She didn't think of Cuthbert or his castles or his wealth. And she didn't think of her sorcerer, with his military jackets and his cloak of lies. She thought of Gabriela. She'd been much happier when that urchin was around, sleeping with the sorcerer in Martha's bed. She never touched the child, though she dreamt of incest the moment she put on her sleeping mask—it was the same as having a daughter in the house.

She couldn't be sure if Gabriela was twelve or twenty-two—a

stranded doe that drew all the creatures out of the dark. Martha had to protect her from these night prowlers, and from the sorcerer himself. It was like having a menagerie in her own bed, full of jungle grass. The wildness comforted Martha, made her feel a little of the wildness within. And in her dreams, Martha was often a jungle cat, a predator feeding on human flesh, with blood and bones in her mouth. She ravaged without mercy, swallowed entire towns—women, children, warlocks and old witches, savoring their fat and gristle.

Martha grew enormous. Children screamed; none could escape her claws. But she didn't spoil her own den. While she prowled and took her plunder of blood, Gabriela snored on the far side of Martha's bed. Gabriela and the sorcerer.

LITTLE RED

−22−

STRANGERS AT MY SALON LOVED TO HEAR how I had been raped on the Orient Express.

"How old were you, Anya?"

"Seventeen."

"Who was your father?"

"A count from Budapest."

"And your mother?"

"A whore with royal blood."

"How many hussars were on the train, Anechka?"

"At least fifty," I said.

And with amazement still in their eyes, they would ask me about Jurek.

"Did he write *The Painted Bird* in this apartment, Anya?"

I stared them down like a Cossack.

"Your Anya is not a stool pigeon. I cannot betray the trust of a friend."

But imagine what I could have told them.

I was Jurek's muse—more than his muse. I was his heartbeat as a writer. I live a block from the apartment-palace where he once lived with the petroleum jelly heiress, Martha Will. I knew him long before he met Martha. And I knew him after she died—was it '68?—with a murderous marriage of alcohol and prescription drugs that Martha herself mixed. She'd suffered from blackouts and deranged fits, and was locked away in clinics time after time. Jurek hinted that she'd had a brain tumor. But there were no tumors. Her brain was pickled, poor thing. My Marilyn had also died of an overdose, even if a lot of troublemakers will tell you that it was the Kennedys who killed her.

I first met Jurek in '57, and he was fresh off the cattle plane. Another Polish dissident, with a million more like him waiting to be let out of some closet that the State Department kept with its own key. But Jurek was different. He didn't stink of oily fish, didn't blab about Stalin's crimes. He had a boy's undeveloped body, but with knees as sharp as knives. He had pointy shoulders and a breastbone that looked like a sunken arrow. I was fond of all his irregularities. He fit right into my plans with those pointy shoulders and his passion for Dostoyevsky.

I had the beginnings of a literary salon since I'd published a pornographic novel, *Nefertiti's Nights*, about a dominatrix in Manhattan, and it made something of a splash. Jurek was my protégé. He would appear at my dinner parties in his awful muskrat coat and sit with his hands folded while I told stories of my love affair with Marilyn. It was during her "sabbatical" in New York—1955—when she'd dropped DiMaggio and all the Hollywood moguls and was having a fling with Marlon Brando and a secret affair with her married admirer, Mr. Arthur Miller.

"My dears, I'd met her at a party. Dietrich was there. She went up to Marilyn and wiped a trace of lipstick off her cheek. I wasn't that bold. I was trembling. It was Marilyn who bumped past me and whispered in my ear. 'I'd love to dance, but it would drive all the men crazy. And if I went into the toilet with you, and we did it in the tub, Lolly Parsons would bitch about how Marilyn went to Manhattan to become a dyke. I'm not dykey. I happen to like your

mouth.' I swear to God that's what she said. We went to my place.
She didn't even give me a chance to lock the door. She bit every
inch of my body. 'Anya,' she said, 'you bring out the devil in me. I
could never be that aggressive with a man. Arthur fucks like a little
boy. He wants me to meow every time we do it. But I wouldn't
have to meow with you.'"

That's when I'd usually start to sob. The memory hurt like hell.
And it was Jurek who came to the rescue, like a relief pitcher with
his own fireball. He told of the atrocities he'd suffered as a little
boy wandering through Poland. There wasn't a moment of self-
pity. The stories spun out of him like a perfect piece of thread.
But I had no perfect pieces. I would see Marilyn in my mind's
eye, feel her fragrance, the sweet smell of her skin, and I was
paralyzed. That's when Jurek would serve the chicken paprika,
toss the salad, and entertain.

—⁓

SOON JUREK SEIZED HOLD OF MY DINNER PARTIES, and I was
stuck with tales of Marilyn I couldn't seem to tell. It was as if
Jurek was thinking in chapters, in swaths of connected material.

"You must put your adventures into a book. I insist. There's
nothing simpler. I'll help you, Jurek. Didn't I scratch out *Nefertiti's
Nights* in one or two sittings?"

"But Anechka, I can't write a word in English. It's hopeless."

"Don't write—talk! And I'll take everything down."

"I'll sound like a man on a tape recorder, confessing to the secret
police."

But he already had a lesson plan—his "Novak," nonsense about
the Soviet Union that he'd scribbled in Polish, and had one of
his mistresses, a fellow dissident, translate. Then a freelance editor
helped him prune the prose. He named himself after Kim Novak,

the Polish-American bombshell, who was nothing, a cow with bleached hair, next to my Marilyn.

But Joseph Novak had the song of a wandering sociologist. Jurek had to find a voice that wasn't cluttered with jargon. He had to descend deep enough to pluck this voice from his entrails.

"I'm not Turgenev," he groaned. "I am faceless, Anechka. I have no style."

"Then find one, and don't whimper to me."

But he was occupied with a widow he met in 1960, Martha Will. He married her two years later on a whim. He got rid of his Polish friends, and Jurek became "Jerry," a newly minted American cockatoo who performed for his wife's rich friends. He traveled with the widow, went to Florence and the Far East. He told his orphan's tale to an editor at a Boston publishing house, who happened to be one of Martha's dinner guests. And suddenly he was back at work.

He devoured books about other lost boys in Poland. He took endless notes. He would come crying to me.

"Anya, I can't write."

"You don't have to be Turgenev. Be yourself, Jurek."

"But I told you. I am invisible on the page. I am like an amnesiac. I don't even know who I am."

"That's an advantage," I said. "Write, or I'll break your bones."

He finished a draft, wrote the book again. He hired a Polish slave to translate it for him. But the book was chaotic, without a fine thread. The charm of his narration wasn't there. And the two of us fished around for "ghostwriters" who could locate the thread that Jurek had lost in the writing. We gambled on poets, professors, and philosophers short of cash. But we never stuck to one. We wanted *our* "ghost" to reimagine the voice of a boy who had become a sleepwalker and could recite the horrors around him with detachment and precision, the precision of shock.

I didn't have that kind of genius, and neither did Jerzy. His stories spun out of control on the page. It wasn't a morbid fear of the written word. He was a man caught between languages, who had no real language of his own—all his texts were "translations" of the subtle, snakelike music inside his head. He told his stories to our friends as if he were on some deck, observing a boy who might have looked like Jurek but was all alone and had to fend for himself.

The editors we hired brought us closer and closer to that boy, but they couldn't recapture him. They couldn't charm the snakes in his head. Jurek basked in his Polish gloom.

"Anechka, I'll shoot myself today or tomorrow. You'll have to bury me."

"Why? You have a rich wife. Let her bury you."

He'd married Martha with the same detachment of someone who was narrating his own life at a distance. Did he love her? He wasn't as interested in her money as his enemies like to think. He loved her as much as his own relentless scheming would allow. He cared for her when she was ill, but he never gave up a single one of his mistresses for Martha. And she couldn't cure his own ills over a half-written book that seemed to wander like a chicken without a head. We were also headless chickens, Jurek and I.

And then we found Gabriela.

$-23-$

S HE WASN'T EXACTLY A FUTURE FLOWER CHILD. She'd grown up in an orphanage, the ragged love doll of older orphans and sadistic, unwashed keepers, and still managed to finish high school and spend a year at Bard College on a full scholarship. But Gabriela couldn't sit still. She ran away from college with a fifty-year-old farmer and was caught soliciting seniors (women and men) at a Golden Age center. And that's when I got an SOS from my own lawyer about Gabriela—his second cousin, he insisted—who couldn't be released from the Women's House of Detention until someone "chaperoned" her out of that stinking jail.

Jurek was kind enough to accompany me—he was also damn curious. We pretended to be a married couple for Gabriela's sake. We planned to chat with her, buy her a meal, and put her on a Greyhound bus to Iowa, where she supposedly had a stepsister. But all our plans went into the toilet.

I could blame it on that rotting hulk behind Jefferson Market. Inmates screamed from its grim walls. Their lament chilled my bones. It was worse than a lunatic asylum inside. Women with marijuana twisted into their hair hopped around in ankle bracelets. Nurses and guards had the torsos of football players. I had to show my birth certificate to Gabriela's jailors, swear that I was her aunt. It took the guards half an hour to find her.

We soon understood why. None of the guards or inmates could bear to part with Gabriela. She was a tiny waif with tits. Her eyes were hazel and seemed to glow in the jail's sinister light. Her hands were as crisp and volatile as a child's. She wore a simple smock, but it couldn't hide the delicious curve of her belly. Her hair was a reddish brown, like Marilyn's, before she went to Hollywood.

Gabriela was as shy with us as we with her. We had pasta and wine in the Village. She stroked our hands while we ate and harrumphed like a frisky horse until Jurek wiped the red sauce from her chin. Then she lay with her head in my lap.

"I'm sleepy, Auntie Anya."

We couldn't abandon her to the bus terminal. We were both in love with that sultry little bitch. We brought her back to my place in Jurek's Lincoln Continental. I tried to be a good Christian, but I trembled with un-Christian ideas as I imagined her a milkmaid trapped in a labyrinth of rosebushes with prickles that tore into her flesh. I lapped her blood like a lamb.

We put her to bed in my spare room. Jurek and I sat at my desk and picked our brains, trying to solve the riddle of that abandoned boy in his book, to give him a voice that would keep his adventures from lapsing into random wisps of chaos. We worked for hours and accomplished very little.

WHEN JUREK AND I AWOKE, the little bitch wasn't there. I panicked, thought she'd run off with the five hundred dollars I kept in a shoe box. But she sat hunched over my desk, with one of the green pencils Jurek always used because his "spiritual father," Josef Stalin, liked to edit with a dull green pencil whatever manuscripts that Soviet masters submitted to him. Jurek would boast that Russia had one style under Stalin's reign—the broad, masculine strokes of Stalin's green pencil.

But Gabriela had her own miraculous style. Because she herself had been abandoned and abused, the abandoned boy of *The Painted Bird* must have seemed like her own lost twin. And with little strokes—a word and a line here and there—she restored pieces of the missing thread.

Gabriela worked on instinct alone. She couldn't shape Jurek's book, only catch idle threads and pluck them out with her green pencil. She proceeded in fits and starts, whenever she wasn't seducing us. She had no sense of time or belief in a career, not even a wish to travel. I couldn't really tell what Gabriela wanted other than to bewilder her new uncle and aunt and scratch away at Jurek's book. The sound of the pencil seemed important to her. She had to hear its rip across the page. And God forgive me, but I wondered after a while if her editing was a diabolic response to the violence that had been visited upon her, if it was a kind of rape.

I repeat this because I was utterly confused. We were both sucked into the storm of this child. We couldn't keep our hands off Gabriela.

"Jurek," I whispered while she was asleep. "We have to stop. It's practically criminal. She's been abused, soiled by ogres, and we're keeping her as our concubine. We have to stop."

"I know."

He was miserable. I don't think Jurek had ever been in love in his life until we met Gabriela. He'd always been the seducer, the ringmaster of all his little love plots. He hadn't trapped Martha into marriage—it was her own idea to rebel against the Manhattan blue bloods who had scorned Jurek—but he'd captured her in his spiderweb, had wooed her like a tarantula. And now he barely slept in the same bed with her. He was bored with her apartment-palace. He couldn't be away too long from Gabriela's glorious stink.

Even if we'd steeled ourselves and had made peace with God and the devil, we couldn't have tied up Gabriela and put her on a Greyhound bus with some small inheritance. She would have landed in worse trouble. And how could we swear not to sleep with her?

"Anechka, I'll give her a salary—to help me write the book."

"But where will she live?"

"With Martha and me. We'll adopt her."

"Jurek, she's twenty-one. And you can't have part of the package. I go wherever Gabriela goes."

"You're being childish," he said. But it didn't matter. We had little sway over her. Gabriela did whatever she pleased. She never spent the salary Jurek paid her. She never seemed indifferent to our touch. I thought of Marilyn, who had to meow for Arthur Miller. And I wondered if Gabriela's meows were just as forced, just as brittle. But it would have taken a rocket scientist to read Gabriela's heart. Perhaps the ogres had torn it out of her and left a ticking machine.

She literally liked to walk all over us. We couldn't even rest after our long cuddles. She would climb on top of us with her tiny feet and balance herself on the narrow wall between my tits or hop like a spider from Jurek's kneecaps to a shoulder, his or mine. She never favored one of us over the other, and was careful to give herself equally to our abandon. But I never saw much abandon in Gabriela, with her measured meows.

—24—

〜

IT WAS GABRIELA WHO SCULPTED OUR GAMES with her own
dark sense—her void had been as deep as Jurek's. She was
Little Red Riding Hood and we were the Wolf, disguised as her
uncle and aunt. But Gabriela was much more satanic than the
Brothers Grimm. *Her* Little Red Riding Hood was a temptress
and a terrible tease. And the Wolf, split into two personas, had
no wish to harm her.

We had to stand naked in front of Gabriela like a pair of raw
recruits while she, wearing a cape and hood from my closet,
plucked at our skin.

"Uncle Wolf," she said, "why have you come to Auntie's
house?"

"To worship every inch of you, my dear."

"That's not a good enough reason. You should have planned at
least a little bit of malice. I order you to bite my nipples."

"I can't, my love," said Jurek. "My teeth are too soft. They'll
fall out at the first touch."

"Then you should have worn your dentures, Uncle Wolf. Bite
my nipples."

I could have stopped the game, slapped her once, and she
would have been finished with Little Red Riding Hood, but I

never did. And I had to watch Jurek unravel as she pecked at him like a chicken hawk.

They'd entered some terrible void where I couldn't go. I was out of my depth. Even *Nefertiti's Nights* had a soft, sentimental heart under its debris of detail. But Jurek went into the darkness with Gabriela. And it was twice as dangerous for him, since he loved her. His tenderness could twist him into something not so tender.

Meanwhile, he played the Wolf, or at least his half of our duel persona. He snuffed her nipples with a violent jerk of his nose.

"Little Red Riding Hood, you smell like a peeled peach—no, a brat who terrorized a whole jail with her beauty and would like to make mincemeat of a poor defenseless wolf. But I've been to the same forest, my dear. I had a drink inside your well. I tasted the water, and it wasn't sweet."

"What was it, then?" Gabriela asked. He was sucking her into a whirlpool—his own malevolent imagination.

"It had the sour taste of a witch's menstrual blood," he said.

"But witches don't have periods, Uncle Wolf, and neither does Little Red."

"Then what do they have, my dear?"

"Garlic in their blood . . . and gall. They have learned to fester in patience, to rot a million years before they strike a blow."

The Wolf had a benumbed look. His head must have been reeling from the cruel drama of the trap that was about to spring.

"And what is that blow?" he asked in a shaky voice.

Little Red snorted with the bitterness of a girl who had survived institutions and ogres.

"It's not the blow itself, Uncle Wolf. It's the anticipation. . . . It wounds you and eats your entrails long before the million years are up."

Jurek sniffed his own despair. The Wolf of the Polish forest couldn't defeat Little Red with all his learning and his language games. She started to laugh and whip her head until the hood fell off. But something deep within the Wolf must have snapped. He clutched Gabriela by the hair—like a lunatic angry at a doll. I didn't stop him. His shoulders shook. Tears streamed down his face. I had never seen Jurek cry.

M Y Marilyn had died of an overdose the same week Gabriela did her number on us with Little Red. I moped and cried and wasn't capable of looking after her. She moved with Jurek into 740 Park as his green penciler. I was out of it for a month.

It was Jurek who cared for me, who washed my face and fed me sandwiches.

"How is Little Red? Has she run away?"

"No, no. Little Red is fine."

Martha had had an alcoholic fit and was drying out somewhere in Connecticut; Jurek coaxed me across the street to visit Gabriela. I dreaded walking up that marble staircase at 740. He'd put Gabriela into a room of her own. The Wolf had tamed Little Red—it was worse than that. He'd sucked the life out of Gabriela. Her hazel eyes were sallow. She twitched whenever he talked. He'd become the ogre who didn't react at all, except with icy commands.

"Little Red, you haven't washed yourself today. What will Auntie Anya think of such a smelly girl? Do me a favor and ask Stanislaus to prepare your bath. It has to be the right temperature, my dear. You might scald yourself."

I lit into him the moment she left the room.

"Are you proud of yourself, Jurek? Playing the Prince of Darkness. She's not your little automaton."

"Gabriela's free to go. She could always run away."

"She never runs away," I said.

"Ah, but didn't she run away from college with a decrepit farmer?"

"No," I insisted. "She traded one institution for another. That farmer must have been familiar to her. He must have ignored her when he wasn't beating her up."

"Do we abuse her here? Do we beat her up? Ask the butler. We treat her like a little queen. And she hasn't lost the art of her green pencil. She's edited the whole book, my dear."

"Then show her some kindness, Jurek. Let's celebrate. We'll have a dinner party at the Rainbow Room."

"Impossible," said the Prince of Darkness. "She doesn't like to eat in restaurants. She never learned how to navigate with a knife and fork. Haven't you noticed?"

He twisted his head away from me and spat like a snake, "Darling, come here!"

I heard the patter of her feet. I know I have all the clumsy baggage of a pornographer—but I swear to you that it was like the sound of an angel treading on Martha Will's hardwood floors.

She appeared without slippers, wrapped in one of Martha's robes—the robe was much too long, and its skirts trailed behind Gabriela.

She clung to Jurek, as if wed to him by some invisible string.

"Auntie would like us to go with her to the Rainbow Room— it's a restaurant right in the sky. You can have wisps of cloud in your soup."

Gabriela snorted at the idea. "I might choke on the clouds,

Uncle Jurek. I'd rather eat here. Uncle Stanislaus gives me all the ice cream I can swallow."

"And what's the flavor you like best?"

"Chocolate swirl. May I go now? Uncle Stanislaus says the bathwater will get cold if I linger too long."

She returned to her tub without even glancing at me once.

"Anechka, are you satisfied?"

I didn't answer. I ran past Jurek and out of his apartment-palace, certain I'd never see him again.

−25−

~

I SHOULD HAVE PLOTTED Gabriela's escape, conspired with the butler or Martha Will, but I was paralyzed. Jurek still had a hold on me. Perhaps Little Red had been right about us. Jurek and I were part of the same creature, Uncle and Auntie Wolf.

But the Wolf knocked on my door a month later. He hadn't shaved. He was inconsolable. Martha had returned from the sanitarium, had seen the state of the child, and got her out of "prison" at 740 Park with the butler's help. Jurek threatened to call the police and swear out a complaint against Martha and her accomplice for having kidnapped Little Red. But Martha looked into his eyes with her own conviction. And Stanislaus thrashed the Wolf, who had to hide in a closet.

"Anechka, you cannot understand my humiliation. I had once thrashed my own father, after the war, while we were living on Senatorska Street, in Lodz. He, too, had to hide in the closet. He, too, was terrorized."

"Jurek," I said, but not before giving him a bagel and some strong black tea. "The butler should have beat your brains out. You deserved it."

"I know. That's what kills me. And I'll go to the grave with the memory of my poor papa cowering in the closet. . . . Anechka, you must help me find Little Red. I'll give you all my royalties, what-ever the book will earn, after it's published."

"I don't want your royalties. Gabriela is better off without you."

"Then I'm lost—a blind man who stumbles all over himself, craving her smells."

"But you could have been nicer to her, darling, and she'd still be with you on Park Avenue."

"Nice," he said, "when have I ever been nice? I would have drained all her blood if I'd had the chance."

"And that's what you mean by love?"

He wanted me to seduce Stanislaus and pluck Gabriela's address out of him. I slapped the Wolf.

"Jurek, you're a contemptible man."

He kissed my hand.

"You should be shot," I said. "You took poor Gabriela and turned her into your prisoner and your slave."

The Wolf snickered at me. "*Poor Gabriela.* I was her slave, and so were you, my darling Anechka."

"And suppose it's true. I'm not going to help you. Suffer, you son of a bitch."

The Wolf kissed my hand. He was, after all, quite clever. And we did have our love for Gabriela to bind us, and the book also bound us to her. There were other editors. And then he spent a year reshaping what the reshapers had done. There would be a brouhaha long after the book was published, nailing Jurek to the wall, but God is my witness that *The Painted Bird* was his—and mine.

The "ghostwriters" couldn't have conceived the book, couldn't have invented its starkness or its glimpse into hell. But Jurek courted his own catastrophe. He wrote *The Painted Bird* as a fic-tional self-portrait, but the book's earliest readers felt that it was too harsh, too baroque. They wanted *The Painted Bird* to be the factual story of a Holocaust survivor. He should have screamed and let it remain a book out of Hieronymus Bosch and his own wild imagination. But he let it fall into the realm of a survivor's manual. How could the book fail with its false patina of *lived* events? Who cared about all the obvious inconsistencies? The Holocaust orphan whose parents were still alive. The Catholic boy who was mistaken for a Gypsy and a Jew. His own publisher was suspicious and tried to bury the book. But they hadn't expected such an avalanche of ecstatic reviews.

Jurek himself went into the whirlwind, became the "ghost" of that boy in *The Painted Bird*. And he didn't have Gabriela to be his green pencil, to dig into the underbelly of his prose and stitch what had to be stitched. But I'm not sure that even her green pencil could have saved him. My poor Jurek became Tartuffe, filled with pious little lies about himself. It was the great disease of his life.

I met his mother, whom he had conveniently kept behind a curtain. She came to see him in 1963. It's not that Elzbieta contradicted Jurek's fantastic tales about the war. She never did, but there was still a sadness in her dark eyes.

She had become Jurek's silent clown, nodding here and there in the middle of his horror stories—stories that had obliterated her, returned Elzbieta to the shadows. No one dared talk to her while Jurek wasn't in the room. Elzbieta was his prize, his prize alone, and I wouldn't have risked the Wolf's wrath. But it was Elzbieta who sought me out, smoked a cigarette with me, while Jurek was telling guests how he had caught a German soldier copulating in the forest with a farmer's wife.

"I was this close, a hair away. Had I been his barber, I could have shaved his skull."

"Jerry," said a drunken playwright who was the star of my

literary salon. "I thought all German soldiers liked to fuck with their helmets on."

Jurek laughed that diabolic laugh of his. "Not this soldier. He was very polite. He put his handkerchief under the enormous fanny of the farmer's wife."

And that's when I saw Elzbieta wince.

"Anya," she said, "where were you born, please?"

"I was born in Budapest."

"With name Anna Karenina?" Her sadness seemed to lift for the first time. "I am reader of Tolstoy. How I suffered with Karenina. She was not lucky woman—with men."

I was reluctant to admit that "Karenina" was my nom de plume, but Jurek must have told her I was a dominatrix whenever I could spare the time from working on various sequels to *Nefertiti's Nights.*

"Karenina should have whipped husband and lover and lover's horse, Frou-Frou. Tell me, Anya, did you ever whip my son?"

Elzbieta had made me blush. "No, I never . . ."

"He should be whipped, twice a day, in America."

~

I T WAS THE FIRST AND LAST CONVERSATION I ever had alone with Elzbieta. I'd misjudged her. She was neither Jurek's puppet nor his clown—a reluctant accomplice, I'd imagine. Nor was she as invisible in Jurek's book as might seem at a glance. *The Painted Bird* wasn't Jurek's dialogue with the devil. It was, in fact, a dialogue with the dead. The boy's absent parents are what really haunt the book—they are its ghosts, not the cruel farmers, the mad girls, the partisans, and the priests. They are whom the boy mourns without ever knowing it. They are its missing thread. And Gabriela must have uncovered it with her green pencil.

There's little point in asking what might have happened had

Gabriela *penciled* his other books. They did not have that ghost-like presence of *The Painted Bird*. I'd read them all, labored over them with my meager pencil, fought with Jurek's other "ghost-writers." Some of these books were adored and sat on best-seller lists. But they did not dance in and out of the same darkness. They rarely danced at all.

His legend grew and grew. He ran with Roman Polanski, whom he had known from the student cafés in Lodz. "Romek" was another painted bird—a Jewish Gypsy torn from his parents during the war—who had to dodge the bullets of German officers taking target practice in Cracow or God knows where. But Jurek was shameless after Romek's wife was murdered by the Manson cult family in 1969. He would have died with her, he said, if his luggage had not been put on the wrong plane. He had thrust himself into the murder of Sharon Tate, when he should have kept his mouth shut.

And he clung to his own myth—the Gypsy look-alike who wandered through the war in escapades out of Bosch. But stories began to leak, dark whisperings—his real name wasn't Kosinksi. It was Lewinkopf, and the only wandering he had done during the war was with his parents, members of the Jewish bourgeoisie in Lodz, who took on Catholic names and identities in order to survive. Jurek Nikodem Lewinkopf, now Jerzy Kosinski, was baptized and became an altar boy. He had to hide his penis, learn to pray in Latin.

But that was long ago, in another land. As a literary lion whose face had become its own familiar country, he went on denying what could no longer be denied. And even worse, he invented new lies. Playing polo with his rich friends, he reminisced to journalists how Soviet cavalry officers had taught him a primitive version of polo at the end of the war. And then a horse trainer appeared and said that he had given Jurek riding lessons in Central Park.

It wasn't all frivolous, all bravado. As president of American PEN, he delivered that organization from a diet of tea parties and championed writers who were imprisoned in the Soviet bloc. He was fearless. He would scribble notes to heads of state—I was his unofficial secretary and had to correct his grammatical errors. Did it matter that he sometimes left out a definite article and that he spelled like a bandit? He defended writers with the force of a commissar.

But even that was finally another mask he wore—and Jurek careened out of control. He gave interview after interview where he encouraged journalists to talk about him as another Conrad, someone who had mastered all the illogic and lyrical leaps of a borrowed language. And then the ax fell. Two journalists from *The Village Voice* had been snooping around in Jurek's own secretive barrels and were conducting a witch-hunt, he said.

"That pinko paper is after me, Anechka. They want to ruin my reputation. They can't forgive me for being Henry Kissinger's friend."

They even had one of their researchers interview me. An evil little man, a gnome who looked like Roman Polanski. His name was Max. I wasn't obliged to talk. But I had my own strategy. I would prove to Max that no one but Jurek could ever have written *The Painted Bird*. Hadn't I hired the "ghostwriters," marshaled them like a little army? But Max didn't ask me one question about Jurek. He even took liberties, called me "Anechka," asked me every sort of personal question.

"I was born in Budapest," I said.

He laughed in my face.

"Budapest in the South Bronx."

I thought I would freeze to death—that's how fast my blood pressure dropped.

"Anita Goldstein of Hoe Avenue. The toughest girl on the block . . . you're a Bronx Bagel Baby."

"Shut up, or I'll bite the Adam's apple out of your throat."

"I'll bet you would. . . . Why should I trust anything you tell me, huh, Bagel Baby? You're as big a fraud as Mr. Painted Bird."

And that gnome left with his malevolent laugh.

I *was* a Bagel Baby born in the Bronx, my father a drunken tailor from Kiev. He was also deranged. When he wasn't molesting me, he was beating up my mother, threatening her with the sawtooth scissors he used to cut cloth. I dreamt a million times of murdering him with the scissors. But I never had the chance. The city put him away; he died in Bellevue, after staring at a wall for twenty years, my poor papa. He kept asking for me. I broke down and visited him in the mental ward. I let him feel me up; that's all he had left, the touch of his fingers.

But I swore I would get out of the Bronx. I quit high school and went down to the Village. MacDougal at Bleecker was the center of the world, with its corner cafés. I was partial to the San Remo. The unwashed, unwed poets who drank bitter coffee and wine at the San Remo looked after me. I was their Bronx Bagel Baby. I fell in love with one of the unwashed poets. Her name was Marie. She was a stickup artist and a whore when she wasn't reading her poems at the San Remo. I lived with her for five years. But that's another story, and it doesn't have much to do with Jurek.

That article in the *Voice* did him in. Half of it was rumor and hearsay, but it left him with little ground. It produced disgruntled scholars and hacks who swore they had written *The Painted Bird*. I couldn't even protest now that the *Voice* had pegged me as a serial liar.

Jurek would publish only one more book, *The Hermit of 69th Street*, without a single penciler or "ghostwriter." He wouldn't even let me have a peek at the book while it was in progress.

"Anechka," he said. "My *Hermit* will redeem me."

It was tedious. Even I, who loved him, couldn't read it. Filled with footnotes, it took his hero—a pompous replica of himself— fifty pages to get from his apartment to the street. Portraits of Jurek's mother and father appeared in the new novel. But I preferred them as ghosts, like the ghost my papa had become. Had I loved Jurek more, I might have finished the book. But it was an excellent tonic. Reading five pages put me to sleep.

WHILE JUREK HAD PECKED PAGE AFTER PAGE of his opus, the Bronx continued to burn. And then the burning stopped—landlords must have tired of torching their own buildings. Jurek was despondent over the reception of his *Hermit*. Critics either ignored the book or crucified him.

"Anechka," he said. "I need some recreation. Let's go to the Bronx."

I panicked. I didn't want to return to that Sahara I had escaped from fifty years ago. I was still a Bagel Baby at heart. My veneer of Anna Karenina might rub off the minute I stepped onto those mean streets, but I couldn't keep ignoring his somber mood.

"Jurek, I have a confession to make. I wasn't born in Budapest. I come from the eye of that firestorm in the Bronx."

"I know," he said, and seemed to hop out of his own dark storm.

"But how did you find out?"

"I never believed your little escapade on the Orient Express. Those hussars would have trampled you and thrown you off the train. Darling, let's go to the Bronx."

I braced myself and rode into the Bronx with Jurek in his new Cadillac. It was such a conspicuous car. I feared that the street gangs would smash all his lights. And he wouldn't even travel in the afternoon, like a sane person. He had to arrive on Hoe Avenue after midnight. He dragged me out of the Cadillac. There wasn't a house that was left standing on Hoe. I saw nothing but husks and little mountains of debris.

I should have been appalled, but those husks sat right under the moon.

I started to cry. It wasn't out of bitterness. I stopped fearing the Bronx. And Jurek understood my odd exhilaration. He'd returned to Poland six months before, had visited Lodz, had walked the streets of his childhood, sat in cafés. The pariah had become a crown prince. The Poles, who had been suspicious of him and his books, now accepted *The Painted Bird* as a Polish masterpiece. He was mobbed wherever he went. People clutched his hands and wouldn't let go. A police car had to escort him from town to town.

"It was the smells, Anechka. Nothing had changed. I could sniff the memory of my own armpits."

And he wandered in the rubble of the Bronx, climbed the little mountains of Hoe Avenue, the master of whatever hill he cared to imagine.

Meanwhile, I had to watch myself wither. My priceless tits became potato sacks that reached the ground. I'd lost the art of writing porn. Anya had to earn a living—I opened a punishment palace, Nefertiti's Harbor, moved it to different spots, paid off whatever rackets squad was around. Who could have figured that I would be such a roaring success? Even the literary crowd dropped in, all those starving writers from Elaine's. . . .

Jurek was the only customer I ever cared about. And then he was gone. I couldn't stop crying. I remember now; it was 1992, a year after Jurek had killed himself, and I was mounting a revue at Nefertiti's. I must have interviewed a hundred girls. That's how tight the titty market was. No one was hiring. And there she was in her glory. She could still break the heart of an old hag who hadn't seen her in thirty years. Her brow had wrinkled, and a bit of hazel had gone out of her eyes, but she would have turned every head at the Women's House of Detention if it hadn't been torn down.

"Auntie Anya, are you hiring? Or do I have to shake my tail farther downtown?"

"Little Red, this life isn't for you. Getting pinched by geeks in SS uniforms."

"I've had worse," she told me.

I wondered if she could hear the pounding in my chest. But I took my time with Little Red. I didn't slobber all over her. I gave her the key to my apartment.

And she moved in, just like that, without a suitcase or a back-pack. She hasn't strayed. We eat at home or at a little Italian dive on Lex—Gabriela does my bookkeeping. Numbers are her religion. She tells me how much we ought to spend or save. But it doesn't matter where our conversations start—they always end up with Jurek.

"I still love him, Auntie."

"Damn you, girl. Don't you think I miss him every day?"

"But it's not the same thing—that hunger, like I had a wound, a constant leak."

And she fell into a fit of crying, but that fit didn't distort her face or darken the wrinkles. She shed thirty years, and she could have been that waif who walked into our arms at the Women's House.

"I miss him, Auntie. I miss him a lot. I guess he had a way of crawling under your skin."

"Oh, he was a master at mixing up kindness and cruelty. Did you ever write to him, child?"

"No, but I read his books, and I liked to think of them as love letters."

"That's funny," I said. "I couldn't find much love in his later books. They were loveless skeletons that could have used your green pencil."

"*His* green pencil. I only borrowed it, Auntie. And aren't loveless skeletons a cry for love? We're all painted birds, freaks with our own eccentric coloring, and wherever we fly, the unpainted birds peck at us and drag us to the ground."

"Then we'll disguise our feathers."

"And be like every other unpainted bird? Thank you, Auntie, but I'll keep my color."

She nestled in my arms and bumped me playfully with her crown of short hair. "Painted birds," I muttered, and went to kiss Little Red.

Moses and Gavrila, 1944

$-26-$

They were hiding in the woods, not from the Gestapo or the SS, who seemed indifferent to the villagers and their plight, but from the Kalmuks, who had been unleashed upon them by some invisible German high command. The Kalmuks had plundered nearby villages, raping women and also young boys in their maddening lust, stealing horses, and setting fire to houses, barns, and huts. The Kulmuks had nowhere to hide. They were deserters from the Russian army; the *rosyjskis* were advancing everywhere and would soon be upon them; and he would have to watch the *rosyjskis* rip out their eyes and roast their hearts.

Jurek had recently turned eleven. He feared the Kalmuks, who might rape him, along with the young girls and wives of the village, even rape his *mama,* but he couldn't help feeling sorry for those wild men. He had seen one or two wandering in the forest in their war paint—streaks of red and blue that ran like gashes from their left eyebrows to their chins, leaving them blind in their one painted eye. They had also painted their ponies. And Jurek, who had seen the polished boots and splendid caps and coats of the Gestapo and SS, with silver buckles and lightning bolts, was transfixed by the crazy uniforms of the Kalmuks; horsemen who rode in slippers, wearing torn Gestapo breeches and tunics stolen from Russian officers, they sniffed the wind like hunters rather than common soldiers looking for someone to rob and kill.

Reports had come back from the village, whose elders had to abandon the old, the lame, and the ill. The Kalmuks who fell upon Dabrowa Rzeczycka must have been a sorry lot. They scavenged for food, leapt with their ponies into houses and barns, but they plundered no one. They even fed a starving old woman and played cards with her. Jozef Stepak, boss of the elders and "mayor" of the region, thought it was a trick.

"They are trying to lure us back. We must wait."

"You are wrong," said Jurek's father, Moses, who was called Mieczyslaw in Dabrowa, as part of the village's own game with the Germans. The village didn't dare expose Mieczyslaw Kosinki as a Jew. The Gestapo would have burnt Dabrowa to the ground and sent each villager to a death camp. And so the elders had to shield Moses and his little tribe of Jews, pretend he was a Catholic and a Pole. And Moses didn't even kiss their hands and ingratiate himself to their wives. Rather than hide, he appeared in the village, became a "professor" who offered lessons to backward students, and worked for the village's tax assessor. And now he considered himself one of the elders. It was their priest, Father Okon, who had brought the little tribe here less than two years ago in a Gypsy wagon. They ranted at the priest. "This Jew will get us all killed." But Father Okon swore to the elders that he would destroy the village with his own hands if they didn't hide the *zyd*.

"Father," they said, "we are your flock. You should not speak to us with violence in your heart."

He cursed them, called them pieces of shit—their own priest. They took in the *zyd*. And now Father Okon himself was a renegade, running from the Gestapo. And they were stuck with Mieczyslaw-Moses. He was valuable to them, they had to admit.

Zydek as he was, he could write letters in perfect Polish. And when they had to consult a specialist in Warsaw, it was Mieczyslaw who crafted the letter. It was Mieczyslaw who had a way with arithmetic, who instilled a love of numbers into the numbskulls they had for sons. He didn't tremble in front of German officers and SS men, but spoke to them in their own harsh tongue.

And he contradicted Jozef and the other elders.

"The Kalmuks have no tricks. They are desperate. And their desperation makes them kind."

The elders wouldn't listen to such infernal logic.

"We will stay here, Brother Mieczyslaw."

And so they all waited in the woods, but they were not guerilla fighters who could devour the landscape and steal food from the weak and the lame. Caught as they were between two partisan camps—the nationalist "whites" and the "reds"—while the Kalmuks and their German masters retreated and the *rosyjskis* advanced, the elders of Dobrowa Rzeczycka hadn't been able to scrounge enough food for an entire village; they had to send their own children to hunt for pigweed and wild berries, warning them not to stray into the hands of the Kalmuks.

But Jurek wasn't permitted to join this little party of foragers.

Jozef Stepak wasn't an utter idiot. He understood the children's cruel tricks. They would stuff wild berries down Jurek's throat and call him "Christ killer." Jozef couldn't have cared less about children's games, but what if a German sentry beside the train station heard their taunts? The SS would miraculously appear and wipe Dobrowa off the map. But why did the little *zyd* look at him with such smolder, such heat?

"Mieczyslaw, please, you son is giving me the evil eye. You must tell him to stop immediately."

Jurek turned his head away. He was smoldering. Couldn't he

have been a Kalmuk for five minutes, with red paint in one of his *evil* eyes? He would have plucked out Josef's heart, held it in his hand, and eaten it raw with a chopped onion. How they would have feared him, these villagers! They did not fear his father, but gave him a grudging respect. Moses had joined the red partisans, the PPR, and the whites had put him on their death list. But Moses did not carry a gun or a knife; he walked around clutching a chess piece, a black queen—that was his weapon. He was the very best chess player in the district. He often played with a Polish prince, who had his own castle in Charzewice. They would sit for hours over the chessboard in Moses' tiny apartment at Dobrowa. The SS had taken over the prince's castle, and he was as much of a wanderer as Moses.

And then one night, six months ago, the SS knocked on Moses' door. Jurek's mother was in mortal terror; Elzbieta Kosinska rarely stepped outside the apartment. She looked like Queen Esther, with her full-throated beauty and bewitching black eyes. No one, not even a half-wit, could have mistaken her for anything but a Jewess. And Moses, who had lived by his wits, with false papers, a new name, and a tiny fortune of dollars sewn into his pants, had to hide not only traces of his Jewish past but also his Queen Esther of a wife. She plucked her eyebrows and painted her nails. She read books. What else did she have to do? She was practically an heiress, had come from the Weinreichs, a family with far more wealth and culture than his own. And he had this unconscionable feeling that he always made too much noise in her presence, that he smacked his lips whenever he ate, that his footsteps were much too heavy. He wasn't the Jewish prince that the Weinreichs had imagined for their only daughter. But how many Jewish princes could have gotten Elzbieta out of the scrape of having an SS captain in her foyer?

He hadn't come to arrest anyone. He was a certain Flotner, who had a hunger for chess. He must have heard from the Polish prince, whose castle he occupied, that Herr Professor Mieczyslaw Kosinski was the only reliable chess "companion" within a hundred kilometers, other than the prince himself. He did not wear any medals or death's-head insignias. He wore a modest, unadorned uniform. He'd even brought cognac and cake.

But Elzbieta couldn't stop trembling. The apartment was filled with crucifixes and statues of the Holy *Matka,* but Captain Flotner did not even glance at them. He shook Jurek's hand without taking off his kidskin gloves. Then he smiled at Henio, Jurek's mysterious "half brother." Henio was four years old; he had blue eyes and blond hair, and Moses had picked him up in Sandomierz, after they had fled from Lodz. At first, Jurek couldn't understand why Moses would burden an overburdened family with a stray child. But all Jurek had to do was think of chess. Henio was part of their elaborate camouflage. He had the Gestapo recipe of irresistible blondness. And Moses was using him as his own form of "Sicilian defense" against SS captains and Polish farmers, to hurl them off guard and then mount his own curious counterattack. The invisibility he sought came from moving among his enemies; that's how Moses blended in.

Henio came with his own nanny, a devout Catholic named Katarzyna, who added luster to the camouflage. But Moses wasn't harsh with Henio, didn't treat him as a stepchild. Moses treated him with a tenderness he couldn't seem to spare for Jurek, until Jurek plotted in his dreams to murder Henio. It was Elbieta who saved him, Elzbieta who ignored Moses and Henio and the nanny, and had Jurek polish her toenails while she combed his hair.

The SS captain couldn't keep his eyes off her. He watched her through the amber glow of his cognac. He asked her questions in Polish.

"Madame Kosinska, you must be bored to death in this dreary village."

"I am," she said; now it was Moses' turn to tremble; he worried that the SS captain would stumble upon their Jewish past.

"But surely, madame, you could visit us at Charzewice castle. My wife has learned to make the most elegant Polish dishes. And there isn't one intelligent face to hold her attention—nothing but Polish blockheads. Promise me that you will come."

Moses leapt in. "My wife is tired, Herr Kapitan. She has a rare blood disorder. Nothing fatal. But it is difficult for her to travel—even to Charzewice castle."

It was Elzbieta who suddenly knew how to gamble with this SS man. "I will make the effort . . . for Frau Flotner."

And the chess game began. Moses could have beaten him with his eyes closed. But he had to play into the captain's strengths, let him grab a sudden victory.

"Herr Professor, that was magnificent. I congratulate you. I used every trick . . . but next time please don't let me win."

He picked up Henio, carried him on his back, kissed Elzbieta's hand, bowed to Jurek and Moses, and was gone.

Elzbieta began to scream as soon as Captain Flotner's motorcade left the village.

"Moses, we must run—he knows, he knows. He will be back with his butchers."

But her husband bounced Henio on his knee. "It doesn't matter what he knows. He's lazy. He'd rather play chess than hunt for Jews. But confound that captain. He's a better player than I had figured. He let me think I was letting him win—Jurek, don't you agree?"

Jurek wasn't pondering the complexities of this new match between the SS and his father, or the danger of his mother disappearing into the maw of Charzewice castle—there was none. He was dreaming of the captain's kid glove, so soft it could smooth away the little bumps and wrinkles on his own hand. Jurek no longer cared about a life of adventure as a high-wire artist or a bomber pilot. He wanted to earn enough of a fortune to buy pair after pair of kidskin gloves.

— 27 —

It was the second day in the forest, and their stomachs growled. Jozef Stepak had wild, unpardonable dreams of dining on the flesh of the village half-wit. The children he had sent out to forage had accomplished very little—a fistful of squashed berries and some rotten pigweed.

"Brothers, it's much too quiet. The Kalmuks might have set a trap for us. I will not lend them our wives and daughters."

"I beg your pardon," Moses whispered in the elder's ear. "But the Kalmuks are frightened of the Russians. They have lost their *pępeki* in the woods."

"It's nothing to laugh at, Brother Mieczyslaw. They are vile men, with or without their *pępeki*."

"They are shadows," Moses had to insist. "If the devil does not help them, nobody will."

Jozef and the other elders spat three times and crossed themselves. Moses smiled under the mask of his face. They are ignorant farmers, he mused. Their superstitions weigh on them like shit in their pants. The *rosyjskis* will have no use for the elders of Dobrowa.

But Moses was worried about his wife. It was the first time that villagers had seen much of Queen Esther in the flesh. She seldom had to roam from their apartment until the Kalmuks began to threaten Dabrowa. There had been no roundups in the village.

The German garrison at Zaklików never interfered in the politics of Dabrowa—and the garrison was filled with ghosts now that the *rosyjskis* were less than two hundred kilometers away.

The only other time she had ventured from the apartment was at the little party Moses and Queen Esther gave to celebrate Jurek's First Communion. Elzbieta had been against sending Jurek to confirmation classes in a neighboring village, against his serving as an altar boy, and mingling with other altar boys, who despised him and thought it was the devil's work to have a *zyd* recite the Mass. They were vicious tattletales, she had said. They would tell the Gestapo about the village's Jewish altar boy.

Moses knew that the boys wouldn't tell a soul. They and their parents would be punished for harboring *zydki*. And he had told Jurek time after time, "Son, this is our own secret service, our NKVD. We have to be twice as clever as the Gentiles, or they will scalp us."

And the boy said, "Papa, what does it mean to scalp?"

"To slice off the top of your head. It's a trick of the red Indians in *Ameryka*."

"Papa, the Indians are *komunisti,* like Jozef Stalin?"

Moses had laughed with such force that he had to clamp his fist into his mouth and bite as hard as he could. But he had watched the sadness grow in his son the more he went to Mass and served as an altar boy. It can't be helped, Moses had muttered to himself, as master of the Kosinski secret service. And then he had a payoff at the Communion party—a kind of acceptance, where the parish priest and the altar boys had to welcome Jurek into the flock. Moses wore his "Sunday suit," and Queen Esther wore a stunning black dress she herself had designed while she was imprisoned in the apartment.

The others at the party were in awe of her. They had never seen a woman wear nail polish—a beautiful woman with Queen Esther's ampleness and dark eyes. She served them cocoa in little cups. They had never had real cocoa in their lives, but imagined that it must have been commonplace at cafés in the capital before the war. And now Queen Esther was wearing that same Communion dress in the forest, as if hiding from the Kalmuks was like *another* party.

Women edged away from Queen Esther, while their husbands ogled her. She hummed a Hebrew melody to herself, convinced that no one could hear. But Jurek listened to the song. He wished he could pull a curtain around his *matka*, not that he wanted her all for himself. She called him her little man—but he wasn't a man. He was an eleven-year-old boy locked inside a town that didn't have a circus or an aerodrome or even an arsenal. And he was condemned to sleep in the same room with his mama and papa, while Henio and Katarzyna, the witch who looked after him, slept on the kitchen table.

Yet he still couldn't figure out this sleeping arrangement. He wasn't clever enough, even if his papa had given him a cardboard badge to wear next to his heart, a badge that claimed he was a spy attached to Moses' secret service. But he should have been able to solve the riddle of why his mama's and papa's beds were sometimes together and sometimes apart; Jurek was their accomplice, pulled into this strange tandem. Sometimes he slept alone, or between his mama and papa when the beds were stuck together like Siamese twins, or else he huddled with Moses in one bed, or with Elzbieta in the other. And if he was a spy, well, he could also spy on them. He'd listened to the other altar boys talk about the occult art of copulation, and about the German brothel in Zaklikow, a little makeshift hut right near the barracks; women would arrive in a green bus—*prostytutki* from the Ukraine, with shaved skulls, wearing skirts ripped out of horse blankets.

These altar boys had an imbecilic passion for the *prostytutki* with bald heads, and Jurek himself had grown inflamed. His penis was like a magical serpent that could sleep or suddenly awake. The altar boys had tried to strip him many times, but he'd always managed to escape—no one had seen the punctured serpent in his pants. The lives of his family depended on it. But Jurek was not only a spy; he was a magician who could make the serpent disappear inside a pocket of skin. But he still longed for the *prostytutki*, and wished their green bus would stop in the woods outside Dobrowa. And no matter how long he watched Moses and Elzbieta with his head half under the blanket, he had never seen them kiss or copulate.

He was plagued with the sudden, irrational wish that his mother also had a bald head, and no matter how it excited him, he wished against that wish. He didn't want his mother to leave on a green bus and live in a brothel. But several months ago, he thought it might happen. While his father was in another town on a mission for the local tax office, the SS captain's dark blue phaeton had stopped at the farmhouse near the Kosinski apartment. The captain's driver, who wore a black uniform with a death's-head pinned to his service cap, snarled at Elzbieta in Polish and German.

"Quickly, Madame Kosinska, and bring the boy."

His mother panicked; her eyes loomed like black pellets under the skin. "But he will miss school, Herr Korporal."

"Bring the boy, madame."

She disappeared for a moment behind her screen in the main room; and when she emerged, she was wearing her one black dress and not her housecoat. Her lips were colored bright red. The driver leered at her and muttered, "*Geschmack*, madame—very, very tasty."

Ignoring him, she collected Jurek and got into the backseat of the phaeton—the seat was made of plush Moroccan leather, in dark maroon. Jurek could not recall such extravagance; his bottom sank into the seat with a soft plop. His mother smelled of wildflowers. His father sometimes smelled of mildew and machine oil. He worried that the phaeton would bring them to the German garrison in Zaklikow; he would watch while the barber "scalped" his mother, shaved off her black hair, and sent her to that green bus with the *prostytutki*; would he have to live on board the bus as a kind of brothel boy? It sickened him and made his heart beat like an insane drum.

But the phaeton avoided Zaklikow and bumped onto another road. It had an escort car with a machine gunner, since German convoys were constantly being ambushed on the region's back roads. The partisans—white or red—had grown as wild as Apaches and attacked Gestapo officers and SS patrols at random. And it didn't seem to matter how hard the Germans retaliated, how many villagers they hanged or shot against the wall. Still another Gestapo officer was found dead on his knees, as if at prayer.

The phaeton arrived at Charzewice. Jurek was disappointed in the castle. It did not have a single turret; its walls were crumbling, and its roof had the rigid, ordinary lines of a farmhouse in Dabrowa. But the castle's front room was as big as a battlefield. The SS captain greeted Elzbieta and the boy with his wife and his own boy, Horst, who was Jurek's age and wore lederhosen, like a mountain climber. Frau Flotner had blond hair that blazed in the sunlight seeping through that battlefield. Jurek was in love with her the instant she held his hand. She had his mother's ampleness, but his mother didn't have a faint, almost imperceptible, blond mustache.

"Madame Kosinska, my wife is used to Berlin—yes, the cabarets are gone, and Berlin itself is like a bombed-out brothel, with ration cards that buy nothing but coffee that isn't coffee and meat that isn't meat—ah, but one can still have a conversation in Berlin.

And I promised that I would bring a little culture to this godfor-
saken prince's palace."

"But I might disappoint Frau Flotner," said Elzbieta. "I am not
so *kulturlich,* Herr Kapitan."

"Ah, but you are refined. I can see it in your bearing. You are
not like the other wives of your village, who have the manners
of a sow."

"But they are farmers' wives. They do not sit in coffeehouses.
They have never seen one. You cannot blame them for that."

"Then why are you and your husband in such a desert, madame?"

"The war, Herr Kapitan," Elzbieta said with a brazen smile that
she never would have dared bestow upon Moses. "The war has
made beggars of us all."

"Ah, but we have a momentary respite at Charzewice castle. Do
me the pleasure, madame. Let us have our little idyll."

Maids in starched uniforms brought out champagne and tins of
sardines, with butter and black bread. These were the haughtiest
maids Jurek had ever seen. One of them nearly stepped on his toes.
They smirked at his mother, winked at him, ducked under Frau
Flotner's arms with their trays, and disappeared.

"Whores," said the captain. "How will I find proper maids
in a wilderness? We're at the mercy of Polish animals. They steal
silverware. They smoke cigarettes in the servants' latrine, and
when they have to urinate, they squat in the garden like the animals that they are."

"Father," said Horst, "you could shoot them."

"I have considered that. But suppose their sisters sneak into the
palace. They'll poison our soup. But we mustn't permit them to
spoil our afternoon."

And it was miraculous for the boy—champagne and sardines
on a slice of bread and butter. Elzbieta had no qualms about letting

him drink. The bubbles in the champagne tickled his nose. Elzbieta, the captain, and the captain's wife took turns playing Chopin and Liszt on the prince of Charzewice's grand piano, attacking a particular étude like some relay team while they laughed and guzzled champagne. And the two boys played "horse and master," each one riding on top of the other. Jurek could survey half the palace from the vantage point of Horst's back.

They had to leave before the sun went down and the risk of ambush was too great. But the captain's driver stopped in the middle of the road. He kept leering at Elzbieta and licking his tongue. He climbed out of his seat like an acrobat and sat with Elzbieta and Jurek at the rear of the phaeton.

"Frau Jewess," he said, "I'll let you and your son free if I can have one feel."

Jurek wanted to defend his mother, but he didn't understand the meaning of "one feel." The driver spat his words in a Polish-German patois.

"Madame, we can go into the woods if you like. I'll lend your son my pistol in case the partisans come."

Elzbieta stared back at the driver. "Herr Kapitan will hang you if he ever finds out."

"Hang me? He's too busy entertaining Jewesses—madame, I have to touch your breasts before I die."

The driver reached into Elzbieta's dress with one of his blistered hands. She slapped him so hard that his cheek seemed to squash. He fell onto the floor of the phaeton. A rage gathered under his eyes.

"I'll kill you here in the woods—you and the boy."

Elzbieta slapped him again and beat his crown with her fists. He whimpered and covered his head. He wanted to kiss her hand.

"I'll shoot myself, madame, if you don't forgive me."

She kicked him with her summer boots, thin as paper. He crawled back to his seat and returned Elzbieta and the boy to Dabrowa. There was a smile on his face that Jurek failed to grasp. Had he witnessed some odd copulation that included punches and kicks and could be accomplished without either party removing any clothes? But his mother wouldn't have copulated with an SS corporal.

"You must tell your father nothing," she said. "The visit to Charzewice will remain our secret."

So now he was part of his mother's secret service, but what kind of agent could he have been if he slid past every clue? He had sensed something—the pitiless constitution of the maids at Charzewice, women who were secret assassins in the Home Guard, the white partisans' little army. They slaughtered Frau Flotner and Horst in their beds a week after Jurek's visit, and beat Herr Kapitan's brains out with the sturdy legs of the grand piano.

— 28 —

‿

By the third day in the forest, the whole village had begun to starve. Jozef Stepak had sent his own spies into Dabrowa, and they had found nothing but a few drunken Kalmuks sleeping in a barn.

Jozef interrogated his spies.

"And none of the crones we left behind were raped?"

"Brothers, we did not hear one cry."

Jozef gnashed his teeth. "It's a trap, I tell you. The second we show ourselves, the Kalmuks will rape our women and steal our strongboxes."

Moses was eager to knock some sense into Jozef, but a *zyd* hiding in a Catholic village couldn't bite and elder's ear or pull on his nose. The village would starve to death if it stayed here . . . or fall upon its own kind and eat a brother's or sister's flesh. And Moses knew that the Dabrovans would fall upon a *zyd* first, and his little tribe would be devoured. So he had to use all his cunning, all his wits. And if he should fail . . .

He played out an elaborate pantomime, gathered his little flock. "Come," he said.

"Where are we going, Papa?" asked Henio, his little angel, who could sing and talk and dance at the age of four. He wasn't like that dark-eyed devil of an older son, who contradicted Moses at every turn and conspired against him with Queen Esther.

"We are going back to Dabrowa," he shouted.

The villagers were stunned. They couldn't let a *zyd* who had joined the Polish Workers' Party, the PPR, suddenly become the vanguard of Dabrowa. This Moses-Mieczyslaw was a little too sly. Those wicked red partisans of the PPR were tied to the *rosyjskis,* and who knows what could happen to a village caught between the PPR and the Home Guard? The Dabrovans formed a ragged line and followed Mieczyzlaw at a safe distance.

Moses laughed in some labyrinthine chamber of his heart. He wasn't frightened of Kalmuks who were on the run and had nothing in their wake but German ghost garrisons. So much of their fury depended on the lightning bolts of the SS. But the bolts were gone.

Moses stepped into Dabrowa in his cardboard boots. The village was as quiet as the dead wind after a storm. He did not find the entrails of a single slaughtered cow. A cock crowed, as if it commanded the town. Moses started to dance in the July dust. Jozef thought he had brain fever. The dust flew, and a Kalmuk walked out of the mirage. He had red paint in one eye, and wore no shoes. He was trembling. He fell into Moses' arms.

"Brothers, sisters," Moses shouted. "Are you blind? We have our first prisoner. The poor fellow is starving. Give him some wine."

And that's how Dabrowa came back to life. Farmers' wives went into their cellars and returned with wine the color of black mud. Other women fed the Kalmuk pigweed soup and raw potatoes. One little girl gave him an unripe berry. The Kalmuk was seated in the village square on a simple throne that the elders sometimes used. The square itself was a rotting mound between two barns.

They couldn't converse with the Kalmuk. They were shorn of

language except for their farmers' lingo and church Latin, and a few phrases the villagers had learned from the Russian and German pythons that were squeezing them to death. And this Kalmuk was from another world, where all men were warriors who clogged one eye with paint and let their children grow into wild packs.

But they were wrong. It was the *zyd* who unlocked this wild man. Mieczyslaw had found a way to talk—with his hands, his eyes, and a few words in a Russian dialect that made little sense to the villagers. When they discovered that the Kalmuk had become a Christian, they rejoiced and gave him flowers to wear. He was a farmer, like themselves, had a family somewhere in Siberia. The Germans, he said, had paid him to kill, had sworn that the Polish were a godless people who copulated with their daughters and produced little devils. And the Kalmuks wore red paint in one eye to protect themselves from these devil children.

The villagers were fond of their new friend, but they couldn't hide him here. The *rosyjskis* were coming, and there would be reprisals if a Kalmuk was ever found. They dressed him in a Polish farmer's cap, wiped the paint from his eyes, and sent him out of the village.

They had their own trump card—Moses' wife. She looked like a *rosjanka* with her dark eyes. They put her on the welcoming committee. They dressed their infants in replicas of Red Army uniforms that they had to buy from a tailor in another town. The elders draped Russian flags on the door of Jozef's barn, which doubled as Dabrowa's town hall. They heard bugles in the distance, could smell the smoke of guns. But where the devil were the *rosyjskis*?

And suddenly three NKVD men arrived, dressed like generals in blue-and-bloodred epaulets, and with them was a pudgy officer in Red Army colors, some kind of political commissar.

But they didn't go to Jozef's barn, even though every flag and sign pointed them in that direction. They climbed the steps of the *zyd*'s apartment and vanished within its walls. Who was this Moses? A demon sent to devour them, or an angel who had plopped into their lap?

— 29 —

～

HE SHOULD HAVE BEEN DRAWN to the NKVD men, who were secret agents, after all, with beautiful clapboards on their shoulders. But they were a little too smug, a little too convinced of their glory. And Jurek didn't like the way the three NKVD generals looked at his mother, savoring her in their own minds—it was almost like an act of copulation. But the fourth man, a commissar with a magnificent double chin, did not stare at his mother. He had a kind face. The NKVD generals wanted to punish the whole village for having shielded the wrong partisans, that stinking Home Guard, with their visions of an independent, imperial Poland.

The commissar disagreed. His name was Gavrila. He didn't wear shoulder boards and a starched military tunic. He wore a simple blouse and the boots of a common soldier. But perhaps these generals weren't generals at all. They listened to Gavrila, who smoked *rosyjski* cigarettes that stank to heaven, though his father insisted there was no such place as heaven.

"Comrade," Gavrila said to Moses, "you are on the Home Guard's death list. So are your wife and son."

Moses struck his temples and groaned, and then fell back behind his mask. "But why would they be after my wife?"

"She and the boy visited a certain SS captain at his estate—Herr Flotner. And your wife was seen playing the piano."

"But that's impossible. She never leaves this room."

"Mieczyslaw," his mother said. "I didn't want to upset you, but Kapitan Flotner's men came to fetch us in his car. They insisted that Jurek go with us."

Moses' mouth moved with a mean, raw pull. "You should have refused," he spat at her.

"Refuse the SS, my dear husband—tell me how?"

"But that settles it, Comrade Gavrila," said the tallest NKVD man. "We must make an example and destroy a few of these Polish pests. Then they'll reveal the hiding places of the Home Guard."

"Please," said Moses. "They are good people. They did not betray me to the Home Guard."

"But we cannot guarantee your safety," said the generals. "There are informers in this village."

Gavrila intervened again. "Comrades, this village will not be touched. And Mieczyslaw's family can remain here."

꙳

GAVRILA ASSEMBLED THE ENTIRE VILLAGE in Jozef's barn. The elders were in awe of Moses, who could come out alive from a palaver with the NKVD. But Moses didn't bask in his new glory. He was seething at his son.

"Have I taught you nothing, you piece of manure! You cannot have secrets from your own superior in our secret service."

"Papa, an agent has to take the initiative sometimes. I was protecting mama."

"From whom?" Moses asked with a scowl.

"From you, Papa."

"And who am I? Hitler's secretary?"

Jurek didn't answer. He was listening to Gavrila, who sat on the elders' platform without the elders, but with the NKVD men beside him. The generals looked ominous in their blue-and-bloodred shoulder boards. They hovered over Gavrila, sniffing at the farmers with a strident, superior air.

"My Polish brothers and sisters," Gavrila said, "we have come to liberate you from the Nazi heel. We will not harm you. But you must not interfere and protect the Home Guard. They would like to bring back the old aristocracy, saddle you with some prince or a king. They are killers who have no heart. You must support your brothers and sisters in the Workers' Party, the PPR. They are your friends. The PPR will not betray you."

Moses listened to Gavrila with a claw in his throat. He knew that Soviet agents had infiltrated the PPR, that it was run by the NKVD, but he couldn't survive without the *rosyjskis*. The Home Guard would be squashed into submission, and Moses had to be on the winning side.

This Gavrila went around Jozef's barn in his peasant boots and kissed the farmers and their wives. He was much more clever than the NKVD, who kissed you with a bullet in the head. But Moses would never be able to get off the tightrope he had been walking on ever since he was a baby. He must have been born with talons instead of toes.

Horses were heard in the village just as the meeting was about to end. Some of the farmers smiled under the flaps of their hunter's hats. The Home Guard had come to Dabrowa to "entertain" the NKVD. Jurek was standing near the barn's big door. He could see a member of the Home Guard sitting backward in his saddle, as if he were having a dialogue with his horse's behind. He wore an ammunition belt slung from his shoulder and a captured SS officer's cap. With him were five other partisans, with pistols and ammunition belts: he recognized one of the maids from the castle at Charzewice. She clucked at Jurek.

"Come out, little boy, and bring your whore of a mother and your father the *komunista.*"

Jurek should have ducked back inside the barn, but he stood there transfixed by these warriors, who were much more frightful than the Kalmuks.

"Come out, come out," the woman clucked.

"Quiet," said her leader, the man in the SS officer's cap, who was still communing with his horse. "I shit on that little boy! I want the *rosyjskis.*" And he called into the barn. "Polish patriots, come out of that stinkpot. You have nothing to fear. Bring the Soviet dogs to us. We will not harm you. Show your allegiance to the Home Guard."

The NKVD men sank deeper into the barn, but Gavrila stepped outside in his boots.

The partisan chief clapped his hands.

"Bravo! What do we have here? A political officer. But where is your regiment?"

"They will be here in a minute, brother."

"That's odd," said the partisan chief. "We did not see one *rosyjski* on our ride into the village."

Gavrila smiled. "That's because we told them to hide."

"You're bluffing. We're going to stand you against the wall, little comrade. And we won't send a priest to such godless men. You'll die without absolution, you dogs!"

But Gavrila didn't even shiver. He whistled once, did a kind of dance step, and the partisan chief flew off his horse and landed with his face in the ground. Jurek had heard only the softest of sounds in the distance, like snow falling from a tree—but there wasn't much snow in July.

The other five partisans stared at their dead chief in bewilderment. But they didn't even have time to aim their pistols at Gavrila. Jurek listened to the same soft chirp from the woods that had such a fiendish pull: The five partisans flew off their horses and were dead before they hit the ground.

Gavrila didn't seem surprised. He winked at Jurek, while the farmers crowded near the door. Then two men marched into the village in hats made of twigs like the crown that Jesus wore; they had twigs all over them and were carrying the longest rifles Jurek had ever seen, with pieces of dark cloth wrapped around the muzzles.

The farmers whispered among themselves.

"*Szatański*," they said. "The Russian devils and their sharpshooters."

Gavrila laughed and went back inside the barn.

$-30-$

J OZEF STILL DIDN'T TRUST THESE SATANS and their sharpshooters. The Red Army had raped women in other villages; that's
what white partisans hiding in his cellar had sworn to him. He
curtailed his welcoming committee. The elders locked daughters
and wives in their farmhouses or retreated into the woods. Moses
scoffed at their foolishness. These dolts were not chess players.
They could not even think one move in advance. The *rosyjskis*
were here to stay. The elders could cross themselves and spit three
times, but their incantations would bring them little—it was like
pissing into the wind.

Moses had Henio wear a red banner and wave his miniature
Red Army uniform and a pistol made of wood. The *rosyjskis* adored
him. They carried Henio around on their backs, tossed him into
the air. And Moses could greet Gavrila's regiment without inter-
ference from the elders. He smiled at the red partisans, who were
really Russian thugs—most of them, and the rest were retired
schoolteachers. He shook hands with the thugs, played chess with
the NKVD generals, drank their sour beer and puffed on their
bitter, unbearable *papierosi*. The generals had silver cigarette cases,
papierośniki that had blackened in their pockets during the war.

He couldn't lure Gavrila into a chess game. Gavrila was constantly with his soldiers, tussling their hair, helping them write

letters to their loved ones, protecting the few women in the regiment—nurses and radio operators—from the greedy paws of the NKVD men. The Russians didn't seem to have *prostytutkis* in a green bus like the Germans, and Gavrila had to watch that his noncommissioned officers didn't prey upon the village, didn't offer *papierosi* to young girls. And when he caught a recruit lurking in a farmer's cellar, he slapped that soldier from one end of the village to the other.

Jurek noticed tears in Gavrila's eyes. He didn't even wash his own raw knuckles. "These are good boys," he muttered to himself.

He made time for Jurek, let him smoke half a *papierosi.* They would hike across the hill behind *Jozef's* barn, sometimes with one of the sharpshooters, a shy boy called Mitka, who had picked off the partisan chief from a very tall tree in the woods. Mitka was illiterate, but he had the sweetest voice, and could sing like an angel. He also had a fierce temper, and it was Gavrila who would get him out of scrapes with the NKVD. But whenever Mitka sang, the whole regiment wept, even the NKVD men. He knew only love songs—about blond boys and older women with dark, mischievous eyes.

Gavrila wouldn't let any tanks into town. He didn't want Dabrowa to be overrun with soldiers. But he climbed the hill with Jurek and Mitka, who didn't say a word. Jurek was already out of breath. He couldn't keep up with the two *rosyjskis.*

"Comrade Gavrila, do you have a rank? Are you a general, like the NKVD men? Or an admiral sent over from the navy to fire up a regiment with political zeal?"

Gavrila laughed with his double chin. "You talk like a Russian lawyer, little one."

"I'm not so little. I'll be twelve one of these days."

"The NKVD wear shoulder bars—we wear none. Yes, I do have

a rank. But that is not how you sway an army. The Germans lost at Stalingrad because their generals were in the rear lines. Our generals fight with their claws."

"Was Stalin at Stalingrad? Did he kill Germans with his claws?"

Gavrila spat on the ground. His eyes seemed agitated. "Comrade Jurek, our Little Father would gladly fight at our side. But we would worry about him. And he does not want to put so big a burden on us. No father ever had such love for his children—did you know that Comrade Stalin never sleeps?"

Jurek was suspicious of that devil with the dark mustache who never sleeps and didn't look so different from the farmers of Dabrowa. Jozef Stalin could have traded places with Jozef Stepak, and who would have been the wiser?

"Comrade Gavrila, you must love your Little Father very much."

And Jurek was astonished that a man like Gavrila, who could face the white partisans without a blink, had watery eyes at the first mention of his Little Father.

"Comrade, I dream of him every night. How would we ever have had the courage to deal with such a heartless war machine without our Little Father and the love of the Russian people? . . . Tell him, Mitka."

But the sharpshooter shrugged his shoulders. He could pick off partisans from a treetop but had an irrational fear of talking to anyone, even a boy who understood less of his own language than he did. But Gavrila poked him. Mitka shut his eyes and whistled a few words.

"Little sir, the Russian soil groans every time our Little Father scratches a finger."

Gavrila glared at him—"Mitka, you should not speak in superlatives"—and then turned to Jurek. "He's a sharpshooter, and as such he lives in a world apart from ordinary fellows."

"How?" Jurek asked, insanely jealous.

"They do not camp with us or eat with us. They live in the woods, and steal their food or pluck it from the ground. They have contempt for army cooks. If there is a rabbit within a few kilometers, they will find it, skin it, and suck out its flesh."

"And what will Mitka do after the war?"

"Shhh," said Gavrila. "We train our sharpshooters to treat all men as targets. They have no future outside of war."

"But won't you help him, Comrade Gavrila?"

"I am nothing but a soldier who keeps other soldiers in line."

"Gavrila," said the boy, "won't you tell me your rank?"

"Me, little one? I have no *exact* rank. I fall somewhere between a captain and a colonel."

And he climbed down the hill with Mitka the sharpshooter, wrapped in his own mystery. Perhaps Gavrila was much too important to have a rank.

~

M OSES HAD BECOME A LITTLE KING while the elders were in the forest. The witches and hags of Dabrowa bowed and called him "Uncle Moses." The NKVD preferred him to their own thugs in the PPR. He translated documents for them into Polish. He helped them interrogate German prisoners who wandered into Dabrowa in rags and begged for food; he did not like the Germans, but it bothered him that these prisoners disappeared after the interrogations and were never seen again.

The little king had to relinquish his posts and welcome back all the elders once Josef's spies said it was safe to return to the village. He couldn't risk a war with Jozef. The *rosyjskis* would move on to other towns, and even the red partisans couldn't help him if Jozef decided to cut his throat with a scythe. But Moses had an exalted position now. He wasn't a *zyd* with a fugitive family that the elders had to hide. The *rosyjskis* had more Jews in their army than there were trees in the Dabrowa woods.

The elders saved a seat for him at their own table. He was now Brother Mieczyslaw, their conduit to the *rosyjskis* and the red partisans. They still had secret dealings with the whites. They scrutinized the red streaks in the sky—no streak could tell them what side would win. Moses wasn't a sentimentalist, but the elders had saved his skin.

"Brother Jozef, you must sever all ties with the white bandits."

"They are not bandits," Jozef had to insist.

"But the NKVD *think* they are bandits, and theirs is the reality you have to consider."

"Speak plainly. Will you inform on your brothers?"

"No. But I cannot keep them off the mark forever—not while you hide whites in your own attic."

The elders got down on their knees and kissed Moses' hand. "Save us, brother. We are caught in the middle. The white bandits swear they will kill us if we don't hide them. And the bandits make obscene noises when our daughters bring them cake."

"Then you have little time to spare," Moses said. "Tell them you have a spy among the *rosyjskis,* and that the NKVD men are planning to search every farmhouse from top to bottom."

Thus Moses became the elder whom the elders relied on. And his new status rubbed off on his son. The children of Dabrowa did not dare to taunt him. He walked the streets with a new swagger. He became friends with Lech, a boy who suffered from brain fever. Most of the other children shunned Lech, who had seizures and outbursts of violence, when he would spit at people. He was five years older than Jurek but could never perform the simplest tasks at church or school. He stumbled rather than walked and had no real expression on his face, as if he were lost in a dream that neither God nor the devil could decipher. But Lech had one extraordinary gift—he could tame birds, call them out of the sky with a warbling sound that didn't seem human.

Lech had a fondness for crows. He would capture a crow, put it in a lopsided cage that he himself had built, paint its feathers white with bird lime the farmers had given him, and set the painted crow free. Other crows were curious about this white creature, then cackled at it until it flew away. But even in its isolation, the white crow couldn't survive. It would succumb to "Szatan," a notorious chicken hawk that the farmers could not kill with their slingshots or their pathetic guns. Szatan raided their chicken coops, swarming down from nowhere, and blinded squirrels with its claws. Szatan's wings were not very wide, but its white-and-brown tail was very long and almost served as another wing.

Lech had tried and tried to call Szatan down from the sky, but the hawk remained hidden in the trees. And when it did swoop after some victim, it wasn't vulnerable to Lech's songs. He had lost *ten* white crows to Szatan, and when he wanted to risk an eleventh, Jurek asked him to wait.

"Please. I'll find a solution."

Jurek had no solution. He was stalling for time. He felt more pity for Lech's white birds than he did for most humans. But he couldn't pick his own brains fast enough. Lech had already painted the crow and was preparing to release it, when Jurek saw Gavrila loping through the village with his military case. Jurek was intrigued by this case that Gavrila always carried with him, slung from his shoulder. It was made of some magnificent cardboard that did not wilt in the rain. He would open this case in the middle of a speech and pull out booklets that Stalin had written. And Jurek could not help it if he had been born a spy! He once glanced a shiny pistol inside the case, a pair of binoculars, and pieces of string. But he was less curious about Gavrila's cardboard case right now.

"Comrade Gavrila, you must help us, or Lech's white crow will die."

Gavrila bowed in the middle of his stride, without upsetting the constant swing of his cardboard case.

"Jurek, are you such a brute that you cannot say hello to a friend?"

"We do not have time for hellos, Comrade Captain-Colonel."

Gavrila laughed and thrust two fingers into his mouth. He whistled so loud that Jurek thought his ears would break. Suddenly, Gavrila's sharpshooter appeared behind him.

−31−

MITKA HAD A TINY SCREWDRIVER TO ADJUST the telescope at the top of his rifle. He adjusted the telescope twice, then put the screwdriver into his pocket. It was no more complicated than that. He licked his finger and held it in the wind. He hummed to himself. He had the blondest scalp that Jurek had ever seen. And that's why Mitka had to wear a cap of thorns and twigs while hunting Germans and white partisan chiefs. His blond scalp reflected so much of the sun that German sharpshooters could have picked him off in a second.

But he was hunting hawks today, and he didn't have to wear his hat of twigs. He walked to Szatan's usual forest lair with the two boys and the painted crow. He sat on the ground, placed his rifle onto a metal fulcrum that was like a miniature music stand, and had the two boys crouch well behind him. He was still humming to himself. Lech took the white crow and tossed it into the air. He sang to it, but the crow hesitated, like some cripple relearning to fly.

Jurek worried that it would crash into the forest floor. But it climbed in a sudden frenzy to the tops of the trees. "Szatan, Szatan," Jurek clucked like an incantation, and the hawk must have listened to its name—it sprang from the foliage in a great blur that his eye could hardly catch and then it splattered into pieces, its feathers and guts swirling where the hawk had once been.

That music stand rocked for a moment, but the rifle itself had never budged from its cradle. Its report had been no louder than a muffled clap. But the rags around its muzzle had caught fire.

"Mitka, we'll all burn."

Mitka waved the rifle like a magic wand and the fire went out.

A few of the hawk's twisted feathers had floated down to Jurek. He captured one in his fist; it was very hot. He was about to celebrate their victory over Szatan when he heard a cry that rent his heart; it was like no other sound he had ever heard, a caterwaul from deep within the throat.

Lech stood with the white crow in his hands; it didn't have one misplaced feather, one string of blood. The shock of seeing that hawk explode must have killed it.

⌁

THAT WAS JUREK'S GOOD-BYE TO SHARPSHOOTERS and the Red Army. Oh, they were around a little longer, bivouacking at the edge of the forest while German prisoners fell into the hands of the NKVD. But the white crow's death had cast a pall over Jurek. And he didn't have Szatan or another hawk to fuel his hatred.

Lech couldn't seem to recover. He had borne the deaths of his other birds. But to have *this* white crow die as a result of Szatan's death was too much for him. He stopped painting birds. He was listless all the time. But Jurek could only imagine the sadness and pain behind Lech's blank stares.

It was Gavrila who wanted to convert the entire planet to the beauties of socialism, Gavrila who attempted to shake Lech out of his empty-eyed torpor. A *prostytutka* had come to the Russian camp of her own free will. There were no SS men to trap her inside a green bus. Her name was Eva, like Hitler's *kochanka*. The NKVD had interviewed her first and roughed her up a little.

Gavrila snatched Eva away from them, insisting that even the diabolic SS were too far gone to send a sixteen-year-old *prostytutka* to spy on the Red Army.

But Gavrila interviewed her himself. And it was Jurek's misfortune that Gavrila allowed him to attend the interview. Her face was cut where the NKVD had struck her with the rings on their fists, and Gavrila had daubed the cuts with iodine, which left enormous orange splotches. These splotches only highlighted her loveliness. She had large pink lips and eyes that shone like blue crystal. And Jurek was hopelessly in love with this Eva at first sight—that was his woe.

They all sat at a table in the forest, as if at a summer picnic. Gavrila had given Jurek and young Eva a *papieros* to share. And it inflamed Jurek to puff on a *papieros* from Eva's lips. Gavrila opened his cardboard case and had her read one of his pamphlets in Polish. Eva couldn't read without moving her magnificent lips.

"Do you believe in socialism, child, that we have no life outside the common good?"

"*Tak,*" she said, like a true believer.

"And no one coerced you to come, bribed you, or beat you up?"

"*Tak.*"

"And you understand that *prostytutkis* are not condoned or recognized in the Red Army, and that we cannot pay you?"

"*Tak.*"

"Then why have you come here, child?"

"The Germans butchered my village, *Pan Komisar*. How can a *panienka* repay except with her body?"

Gavrila began to sniffle. This *panienka* had made him cry.

"But you could help bandage our wounded, you could . . ."

"Please," she said. "I am not so good with bandages. I will be a socialist *prostytutka*. But unofficial, not on your record books.

Would you like to sample Eva, *Pan Komisar?* But the little boy must close his eyes. I am ashamed to undress in front of him."

Gavrila couldn't stop sniffling.

"It is kind," he said, wiping his eyes with a handkerchief. "And I cherish your offer—but, you see, I am a proselytizer, like a priest without his cross."

Eva smiled with a gentle seduction that infuriated Jurek, because that seduction hadn't gone to him.

"*Pan Komisar,* I like priests without crosses."

But he still would not go deeper into the woods with Eva, hand in hand. And when he offered her Lech, who was waiting behind a tree with his usual blank stare, she ruffled her nose.

"Is he *kastrat, Pan Komisar,* a boy without a *pepek?*"

"Silence!" said Gavrila. "Comrade Eva, he is your first case."

She laughed now, grabbed Lech by the rope he wore around his waist. He was bewildered but went with her willingly. Jurek watched with burning eyes until his sweetheart vanished with Lech in a tangle of leaves.

"Gavrila," he shouted, "I'm next."

"Impossible. Your father will have me court-martialed."

"I'm next. You're responsible for a whole regiment. What could my papa do to you? He's not even Russian. I'm next."

"Holy Peter! You heard her. She wouldn't even undress in front of you."

"Then why did you bring me here?"

"To sit in on an interrogation," he said. "To have you learn the ways of men and women."

"I learned enough," he said. "I'm next."

And he dashed into the woods, followed Eva's vanishing trail. She must have heard him coming. She jumped out of the leaves, with Lech's filthy blouse covering her nakedness. She had twigs in her hair, but he didn't see a sign of Lech.

"Miss Eva, I am Lech's adviser. I should have what he has. It's only fair."

"Fair?" she said, her nose ruffling like an adorable rabbit.

She slapped his face.

And he knew that he would be in love with her for life.

-32-

H E NEVER SAW EVA AGAIN, and he was furious with Gavrila—
he prayed for some prince who could deliver him and
demand that the *rosyjskis* leave Polish soil. And when he asked Lech
to explain what had happened behind that curtain of leaves, he was
more furious than ever. Lech couldn't capture much with words.
Lech looked at him with those injured, vacant eyes.

"Soft," he said. "She was soft."

"What was soft? Where was she soft?"

"Soft," he said.

And Jurek was furious enough to strangle him, but it would
only have magnified the fever in Lech's brain. He stopped going
to church. He decided to quit school and become a vagabond
like the famous *rysyjski* writer, Maksym Gorky, who was a boat-
man on the Volga. Jurek was sick of forests and barns and the
mewling cries of cats and cows. He might become a river pirate.
He fought with his father, who insisted that the Kosinskis keep
up their Catholic credentials.

"Jurek, it is our way of hiding."

"Papa, I do not want to hide. I want to run."

"But we must go and listen to the Mass."

Moses chased him across the apartment while Jurek shouted,
"*Zydek, zydek,*" and pushed Henio aside in his Red Army uniform.

Even his mother chased him. But he had grown too strong, too supple, having to fight off other altar boys, who had tried to undress him for two years and peek at his *pępek*. But when his mother started to cry, Jurek ran to her and said, "Mama, mama."

And he went to church one last time. But he wouldn't chant the Lord's Prayer or receive Communion. He kept to himself. He read books.

"Papa, teach me *angielski*."

"Why? Are you going to parachute into London with the Polish free brigade? Better you should improve your chess game."

"Papa, I'm tired of chess. Our whole existence has been a chess game. The Germans could never solve your defense. That's why we are still alive. You kept your queen in a blind. But when will we strike back?"

"And reveal ourselves? We will hide the black queen. If I have to be with the reds today, I will be with the reds."

"But Papa, all these hidden maneuvers have exhausted me. I feel like I'm a hundred—when will I have time to be a boy?"

"When all our enemies are in the grave."

"I can't wait that long. I will inherit Lech's fever."

And while he was hibernating in his father's house, he heard a woman serenade him in the street. He leapt with nervous joy. *It's Eva*, he muttered to himself. She has come to ask my forgiveness and invite me into the woods.

He leaned halfway out the window. It wasn't Eva. It was a different *prostytutka*, with a man's shoulders. He groaned inside his head. It was the sharpshooter in a blond wig, with a smudge of lipstick on his mouth. He was very drunk. Mitka must have been entertaining his regiment.

"Come downstairs, little brother. I miss you."

But Jurek ducked under the window and clapped his hands over his ears. What disturbed him most was that he was drawn to the blond wig and Mitka's raw, red mouth.

⌒

THE ENTIRE REGIMENT MARCHED through the village in a dust storm it alone created. Jurek wouldn't whistle or wave any flags. He kept indoors. But after the clatter of the *rosyjskis* was gone, Jurek ran outside with remorse. He hadn't said good-bye to his friends. He was like Szatan, that dead hawk, who could not love or weep, but only devour painted birds.

He was a hawk.

But Szatan could not believe his eyes. He saw Gavrila in a military tunic loping down a hill with his cardboard case. Jurek ran to him. He didn't dare embrace a commissar.

"Gavrila, I thought you had gone—forever."

"Would I desert my Jurek? Brother, give me a kiss."

And Gavrila did not demean him, did not scold him as a difficult child. He kissed Jurek the way two adult *rosyjskis* would kiss— on the mouth.

"You hurt Mitka's feelings. He loves you."

Jurek started to cry. "I love him, too, brother. But I think this war has given me brain fever. Take me with you, Gavrila. I won't be a nuisance. I'll deliver leaflets from your case."

"And would you make orphans out of your mama and papa? They will grieve for you, Jurek."

"Then let them grieve," he said.

"And if you have no heart, how can I trust you?"

"But I have a heart—for you. And Eva. Where is she, brother? Did you hide her in a tank?"

"No," said Gavrila, the playfulness gone out of his eyes. "I could not have her become the secret whore of a Soviet regiment. It was the same as a death sentence. My boys would wear her out within a month. And then the NKVD would have stolen Eva, put her in one of their special camps."

"But Gavrila, at least she wouldn't starve. You might have sentenced her to death by setting her free."

"No," he said. "Our red partisan brothers found work for Eva in an orphanage."

"Your red partisan brothers belong to the NKVD. And even if they didn't, she won't have Gavrila to look after her."

Gavrila tapped Jurek on the shoulder. "Must I protect every stray girl in Poland?"

"*Tak,*" Jurek said.

"Would you turn me into a little saint?"

"*Tak.*"

"But I am a man who belches and breathes like every other man."

"Take me with you."

"And hide you in a tank?" said Gavrila. "You will visit me in Moscow when the war is over. But you must finish school. Do you swear not to run away from your own little father?"

Jurek shivered with the force of his own lament. "Gavrila, I cannot swear. It would be a lie."

He plotted like an NKVD man. He had little remorse about abandoning the village and the mask his papa had imposed upon him—the little Catholic boy who couldn't show his *pępek*. It was time to put on another mask. He would become a fatherless boy, like the little *żyds* who ran into the woods when the Germans raided their towns and villages; these wild boys lived on roots and bark, and they had their own lantern-stoves, perforated tin cans they filled with peat—such *kometki* often saved their lives. They would attach a *kometka* to a long piece of rope, hurl it at gangs of

Christian boys who tried to capture them and collect a "ransom" from the Gestapo or the SS. They could heat a stolen potato with a *kometka,* knock a squirrel from a tree. But it was the light of a *kometka* that ruined them. Farmers could see it flicker in the forest, and so could the SS, who chased them with dogs. Not one wild boy survived the war.

But now the SS was on the run, and Jurek had the forest to himself. He built a *kometka*, baked potatoes on its blackened lid. He couldn't join up with the *rosyjskis.* He was much too small, but he could shadow Gavrila's regiment if he ever found it. That regiment had become his ideal circus. You didn't have to join this circus, just chase after it from town to town.

But his plan fell to nothing. He hadn't counted on his father's ingenuity—Moses had enlisted the NKVD to help him find his own wild boy. They captured him in a forest with the help of his *kometka.* They were very polite.

"How is Gavrila's little friend?"

He was starving, and they fed him grapes from a wrinkled sack. With all his wandering, his pioneering in the forest, his "conquest" had gotten him no further than twenty kilometers from Dabrowa.

He arrived in a NKVD car, like a visiting dignitary. But no one clapped. Villagers gaped at him from their windows with sinister smiles. But he didn't feel shame—he felt nothing at all. Even as Moses ran to him with tears in his eyes, Jurek dreamt of Szatan's wings, of flying far from Dabrowa and finding another circus. And one day he will.